Emmy had to remember all the things she knew better than to lose sight of.

Like the fact that she was in Boonesbury on business. Boonesbury, where she would never choose to vacation, let alone live the way Aiden did.

Like the fact that at that exact moment Aiden Tarlington could have a child of his own sleeping downstairs in his bedroom. A child he hadn't expected to have and might now have to raise all on his own.

It was just that even remembering all that didn't chase away the image of him in her mind.

Tall and muscular. Incredible to look at. Incredible to be with.

And so simmeringly sexy that she could still feel the heat of him as if he'd left an imprint on her.

Dear Reader,

Our resolution is to start the year with a bang in Silhouette Special Edition! And so we are featuring Peggy Webb's *The Accidental Princess*—our pick for this month's READERS' RING title. You'll want to use the riches in this romance to facilitate discussions with your friends and family! In this lively tale, a plain Jane agrees to be the local Dairy Princess and wins the heart of the bad-boy reporter who wants her story…among other things.

Next up, Sherryl Woods thrills her readers once again with the newest installment of THE DEVANEYS—*Michael's Discovery.* Follow this ex-navy SEAL hero as he struggles to heal from battle—and save himself from falling hard for his beautiful physical therapist! Pamela Toth's *Man Behind the Badge,* the third book in her popular WINCHESTER BRIDES miniseries, brings us another stunning hero in the form of a flirtatious sheriff, whose wild ways are numbered when he meets—and wants to rescue—a sweet, yet reclusive woman with a secret past. Talking about secrets, a doctor hero is stunned when he finds a baby— maybe even *his* baby—on the doorstep in Victoria Pade's *Maybe My Baby,* the second book in her BABY TIMES THREE miniseries. Add a feisty heroine to the mix, and you have an instant family.

Teresa Southwick delivers an unforgettable story in *Midnight, Moonlight & Miracles.* In it, a nurse feels a strong attraction to her handsome patient, yet she doesn't want him to discover the *real* connection between them. And Patricia Kay's *Annie and the Confirmed Bachelor* explores the blossoming love between a self-made millionaire and a woman who can't remember her past. Can their romance survive?

This month's lineup is packed with intrigue, passion, complex heroines and heroes who never give up. Keep your own resolution to live life romantically, with a treat from Silhouette Special Edition. Happy New Year, and happy reading!

Karen Taylor Richman
Senior Editor

Please address questions and book requests to:
Silhouette Reader Service
U.S.: 3010 Walden Ave., P.O. Box 1325, Buffalo, NY 14269
Canadian: P.O. Box 609, Fort Erie, Ont. L2A 5X3

Maybe
My Baby

VICTORIA PADE

Silhouette®

SPECIAL EDITION™

Published by Silhouette Books

America's Publisher of Contemporary Romance

SILHOUETTE BOOKS

ISBN 0-373-24515-7

MAYBE MY BABY

This edition published by arrangement with Harlequin Books S.A.

Visit Silhouette at www.eHarlequin.com

Printed in U.S.A.

Books by Victoria Pade

Silhouette Special Edition

Silhouette Books

World's Most Eligible Bachelors
Wyoming Wrangler

Montana Mavericks:
    Wed in Whitehorn
The Marriage Bargain

The Coltons
From Boss to Bridegroom

VICTORIA PADE

is a bestselling author of both historical and contemporary romance fiction, and the mother of two energetic daughters, Cori and Erin. Although she enjoys her chosen career as a novelist, she occasionally laments that she has never traveled farther from her Colorado home than Disneyland; instead she spends all her spare time plugging away at her computer. She takes breaks from writing by indulging in her favorite hobby—eating chocolate.

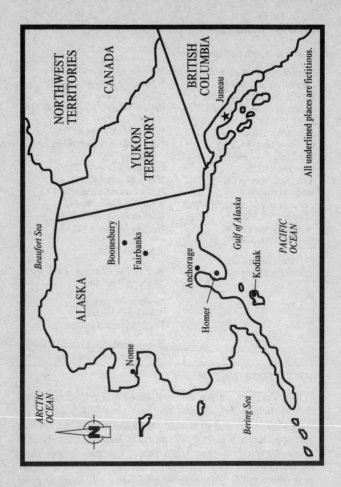

ARCTIC OCEAN

N

NORTHWEST TERRITORIES

CANADA

YUKON TERRITORY

BRITISH COLUMBIA

Juneau

Beaufort Sea

ALASKA

Boonesbury

Fairbanks

Nome

Anchorage

Homer

Gulf of Alaska

Kodiak

PACIFIC OCEAN

Bering Sea

All underlined places are fictitious.

Chapter One

The plane had landed in Fairbanks, Alaska, but there was a delay in clearance to unload passengers. So while Emmy Harris waited with everyone else, she took the makeup bag from her carry-on to do a little repair work.

As the new director of the Bernsdorf Foundation, she didn't want to look travel worn when she met Dr. Aiden Tarlington for the first time. He was a good friend of the head of the foundation's board of trustees—the Old Boys, as Emmy and her assistant referred to them.

The trustees were the seven men—all of them old enough to be Emmy's grandfather—who were her bosses. And if she'd learned nothing else in the two months since she'd been promoted to director, she knew that one hair out of place could shoot a hole in her credibility with them.

So, since she assumed Dr. Tarlington was Howard Wilson's contemporary, she knew better than to present anything less than a perfectly professional appearance and attitude. It was the only way to counteract the demerit of her relatively young age when dealing with that particular generation—even when she was the person in the position of power, the way she was on a fact-finding trip like this one. Which also happened to be her first ever.

There wasn't the need for too much makeup repair, though, because Emmy didn't wear much in the first place. At twenty-nine her skin was clear and she hadn't yet discovered any wrinkles, which meant she didn't have anything to camouflage. She did like to dust her high cheekbones with a pale-pink blush, however, and after a full day on the go she wanted to blot the shine from her narrow, not-too-long nose.

Before she'd left home that morning she'd also applied just enough mascara to darken her lashes and accentuate her hazel eyes. That didn't need refreshing, despite the fact that it was now late in the afternoon. But the pale-mauve lipstick she'd used twice already during the day was once again in need of replenishment, so she carefully filled in her full lips with that.

She'd pulled her very straight, thick, auburn hair into a tight bun at the nape of her neck—again in an effort to add years and professionalism to her appearance. But a few wisps had strayed and she combed them smoothly back into place.

As the plane finally began to roll forward again, she tucked the makeup bag into the carry-on and unfastened her seat belt. She brushed at her navy-blue skirt to rid it of the pencil erasings that had accumulated while she'd worked through the flight. Then she stretched one leg out as far as she could to see if the new, expensive nylons were going to hold up to their claim that they wouldn't bag at the knees even after long periods of sitting.

The minute the plane came to its second stop at the terminal and the pilot thanked the passengers for flying with his particular airline, Emmy stood up and put her suit jacket on over her high-necked white blouse.

She was eager to get off the plane and down to the business of checking out the small community of Boonesbury. Part of her new job as director was to gather information and recommend that the foundation bestow one of their grants to bring more modern medical care to the rural area or recommend that the foundation deny the application.

Either way she didn't want to be in Boonesbury, in Alaska, any longer than necessary. She was a city girl through and through, and she already knew that these trips to the backwaters of America were not going to be her favorite part of being the foundation's director. They definitely hadn't been her predecessor, Evelyn Wright's, favorite part. In fact, a trip like this one, to a very underdeveloped area in Arkansas, had ultimately caused Evelyn to resign.

At the first opportunity, Emmy slipped out of her

row into the main aisle and began the slow trek to the exit door. Aiden Tarlington was to meet her at the Fairbanks airport and take her the rest of the way to Boonesbury where he was the sole doctor.

She imagined that he'd be a paunchy old country doctor and hoped that, if the remainder of her journey required him to drive, his eyesight and reflexes weren't waning the way Howard Wilson's were. The last time she'd ridden with Howard he'd scared her nearly to death.

There were a number of people waiting just inside the gate as she stepped through it into the airport and Emmy initially scanned the crowd for a head of white hair—like Howard's. She had no basis for that. For all she knew Dr. Tarlington might be as bald as Rooney Whitlove—another of the Old Boys.

Then she realized that a couple of people were holding signs with names on them and she amended her view to read those signs since that was a more likely way to connect with the man she was meeting.

No, she was not Sharon.

She wasn't Winston Murphy, either.

But she was Emmy Harris....

Only, the man holding the cardboard rectangle with her name written on it was hardly white-haired. Or bald. Or old, for that matter.

Instead, he had a full head of longish, dark-brown hair the color of bittersweet chocolate. And it was combed haphazardly back from the face of someone more her own age. The jaw-droppingly handsome face of someone more her own age.

Emmy rechecked the sign to be sure she wasn't mistaken.

She wasn't. It was her name written in big, bold letters. And the sign was definitely being held by a man who was not at all grandfatherly.

Maybe he isn't Dr. Tarlington, she thought as she took in the full view on the way over to him. After all, he wasn't dressed to impress, the way the representative of potential grant recipients might be. This man had on a pair of well-worn blue jeans, a V-neck sweater that showed a hint of white T-shirt underneath, and a denim jacket one shade lighter than the jeans.

Not that the attire didn't suit him, because it did. Although Emmy doubted the guy would have looked bad in anything.

He was very tall—probably an inch or more over six feet—and he had about the broadest shoulders she'd ever seen. He also had a very angular jaw: a full lower lip below a thinner, but very sensual, upper lip; a slightly long, slightly hawkish nose; and deep-set, light-blue eyes that would have made him remarkable even if the rest of his face had been plain.

She stepped up then and said, "I'm Emmy Harris," not wanting to address him as Dr. Tarlington since she doubted that's who he was.

Down went the sign and out came a large hand with thick, blunt fingers.

"Hi. Aiden Tarlington."

Emmy barely took his hand, scanning his face all over again.

"*Dr.* Tarlington?" she said for clarification, still thinking this could be the doctor's grandson and namesake.

"Aiden will be fine," he assured her in a deep, rich voice that was all-male.

"*You're* Howard Wilson's fishing buddy?" she asked somewhat tactlessly.

"We've been known to do some hunting, too."

"So, you're friends?"

"We are. Why does that seem to surprise you?"

"I just thought… Well, I guess I just assumed that you would be closer to Howard's age."

"Ah. No, I'm a long way from seventy-two. But we are still friends. And fishing and hunting buddies. If that's okay with you," he added with an amused smile that put tiny creases like rays of sunshine shooting out from the corners of each of his piercing blue eyes.

"It's not that it's okay or not okay. It's just—"

"A surprise," he supplied for her.

"A surprise," she confirmed. "I really did think you'd be one of Howard's cronies."

"Sorry to disappoint you."

Disappointed was not what Emmy was feeling.

What she was feeling was an inordinate—and inappropriate and entirely unprofessional—urge to get her hair out of that bun.

"No, no, it's nothing," she assured him. "You just aren't what I was expecting."

Of course that had been one of Evelyn's many laments—that nothing on these trips ever turned out to be what she expected. But this was hardly something to complain about the way Evelyn had complained about so many things.

"In fact," Emmy added. "It's better that you aren't Howard's age. Now I don't have to worry about being driven to Boonesbury by someone with cataract-dimmed eyesight and not-great reflexes."

"My eyesight and reflexes are fine," the doctor said, and she wondered if she'd heard just the faintest hint of something in his tone that might have been flirting.

Surely she must have been mistaken, she told herself.

Although, those blue eyes of his hadn't left her for a single moment since she'd approached him and introduced herself.

Then he said, "But we aren't driving to Boonesbury, anyway. It would take us a full day to do that and another full day to drive back at the end of your stay. We're flying."

"Oh?" That news confused her, since she hadn't been instructed to book a connecting flight. "And you've taken care of the arrangements?"

"I have. I flew the plane in and I'll be flying the plane out again."

"Oh." There was a tinge of alarm in that one.

Emmy had been Evelyn's assistant for a number of years, privy to the same complaints Evelyn had voiced to Howard about the inconveniences and lack of amenities on these trips. But the final straw for Evelyn had been a flight in a small aircraft that had been forced to make an emergency landing. Emmy had hoped never to be in that same position.

But here she was, on her first time out, faced with flying in a small plane. Piloted by a doctor.

"So you're a doctor *and* a pilot?" she said, trying not to sound as if that failed to inspire her with confidence.

"Licensed in both, yes." He seemed amused again, and there was actually a sparkle in his eyes that made them all the more striking.

Then he leaned forward a little and pretended to confide, "I'm a better pilot than Howard is a driver, if that's what you're worried about."

She was beginning to worry about a lot of things....

"Have you flown much?" she asked.

"Much. It's how I make house calls to see about one-third of my patients."

"Do you own your own plane?"

"Well, let's just say Boonesbury and I are partners in it."

"What kind of plane is it? A tiny prop?" Which was what the other director had had her harrowing landing in.

"Do you know planes?"

"No."

"Then it probably won't do much good for me to give you the particulars, but my plane is a *twin* prop. That means it's slightly bigger than a single engine— I have two engines—and she's a six-seater. A single engine prop would have two or four seats, if that matters to you at all."

"What matters to me is if *she's* safe. I've never been thrilled with small planes."

"She's perfectly safe. I'm a stickler for maintenance, and I've never yet had a single incident that's put me on the ground before I wanted to be."

There's always a first time, Emmy thought. But she didn't say it. Instead she reminded herself that this was all part of the job she was going to do without the nervousness and fussiness Evelyn had exhibited.

Besides, not flying would add two days and who-knew-what other complications to the trip, and she didn't like that idea any better than the idea of flying in a small plane.

So she decided she was just going to have to trust this man.

"I guess it'll be all right," she finally conceded.

"I guarantee it will be."

Emmy took a deep breath and sighed a resigned sigh. "Where to, then?"

"The noncommercial terminal is on the other side of baggage claim. As soon as we pick up your luggage we can head out."

The doctor took her carry-on without comment and pointed with his well-defined chin in the direction they needed to go. "This way," he said.

But even as they began to walk he looked at her, up and down.

"I hope you packed some warmer clothes and a heavy coat," he commented after a moment of scrutiny.

"I have jeans and slacks. And a light sweater."

What she'd thought would cover most needs, even should she have to trek through some countryside.

"No coat?" he asked again.

"It's only September first."

"But this is Alaska."

"Which is why I brought long pants and the sweater."

"The trouble is, Boonesbury isn't far from the Arctic Circle. Our highs aren't getting much above freezing and our lows are already getting down into single digits."

"Oh," Emmy said yet again. She hadn't looked into the possibility of chilly weather because she'd honestly thought it was too early in the season for cold to be a factor even in Alaska. It was still the height of summer in Los Angeles.

But the doctor was unfazed. "Looks like first thing tomorrow we get you a coat and some warmer clothes. Even though it'll be Sunday I think I can get Joan to open up the store for us."

"There's a woman's clothing store in Boonesbury?"

"No, it's more of a general store—Joan sells about everything imaginable. But we all just call it the store."

"I see. Well, I probably won't need much. I'm not all that susceptible to the cold."

Aiden Tarlington couldn't seem to suppress a grin at that. A grin that put two intriguing lines on either side of his mouth. "Uh-huh," was all he said as they reached baggage claim.

It didn't take long to grab her suitcase and get to the terminal used for private flights. Unlike the commercial accommodations, there was no covered boarding ramp, though. They had to go out onto the tarmac. Into air that was surprisingly chilly and hit Emmy like opening the door on a meat locker.

But she hid the shiver that ran through her so her companion didn't see it and have his suspicions confirmed that she was some kind of wimp.

The small plane was dwarfed by its jet-liner cousins waiting at the surrounding gates, and Emmy had a resurgence of tension at the idea of getting into what seemed to her like a miniplane. A miniplane that would be piloted by a country doctor rather than by someone who had made a career of it.

As the country doctor did his preflight check he seemed to know what he was doing, but still Emmy buckled up tight and found both armrests to clutch just for good measure.

Then, after some back-and-forth conferencing with the control tower, they taxied out to the runway and took off.

"We'll be flying relatively low," Aiden explained over the din of the engines. "So you'll get a good look at things until we lose daylight. And in case you were wondering, I am instrument trained to fly in the dark."

Emmy hadn't known special training was required to fly at night, and it didn't help calm her nerves to learn that it did. Even if he was qualified.

"Come on, relax and enjoy the sights," he urged as if he knew what she was thinking.

They weren't in the air for more than a half hour when all signs of civilization disappeared and a spectacular panorama took over.

Aiden began to point out lakes and glacier-made valleys, specific mountain peaks and natural wonders Emmy might have missed otherwise.

But despite the incredible beauty of it all as a setting sun dusted everything in rosy hues, Emmy was left with little doubt that she had entered a true wilderness. And that didn't thrill her. In fact, it left her with a sense of isolation she hadn't thought she'd ever feel again, even on these trips.

To keep the feelings at bay she told herself, I won't be here forever. I'm not changing my whole life the way I was before. I'm only here for work. For a short while…

But still the feeling persisted, tormenting her.

The flight took about an hour and a half—the last half hour of it in darkness. But finally Aiden announced that they were about to land.

"Where?" Emmy wondered aloud since she couldn't see an airport or so much as a light in the distance as they descended. And, unlike on takeoff, there was no radio contact going on, either.

"We'll put down in the field. It's what passes for Boonesbury's airport," Aiden informed her.

"A field?"

"It'll be fine," he said with yet another touch of amusement in his voice.

But the reassurance didn't keep Emmy from hanging on to those armrests with a white-knuckled grip. Or from thinking about Evelyn again and beginning to understand why the other woman had had so many complaints about the conditions she ran into on these trips.

Aiden was very intent on what he was doing, and his concentration allowed him to land the plane smoothly, gliding to the ground with little more than a bump before the plane slowed and came to a stop near a small shack illuminated by a single pole light. There was an SUV waiting beside it but no one was in the SUV. And no one came out of the shack to greet them, either. In fact, there was no indication of another human being anywhere around. There was just the field, the shack and a whole lot of fir trees in the distance.

But at least they were on terra firma again and the relief of having accomplished that without incident was enough for Emmy to once more vow that she would rise above whatever rough patches she encountered.

As Aiden shut down the engines and began flipping levers and noting gauge readings on a paper on a clipboard, he said, "Oh, I forgot to tell you. The bed and breakfast where you were supposed to stay had to close. Their pipes burst. So you'll be bunking with me. And since my cabin is between here and Boonesbury proper—what there is of it—we won't get into town tonight.''

"*Bunking* with you?'' There was enough of a surplus of shock in that to completely hide the fact that something like titillation had taken a little dance across the surface of her skin at the idea of ''bunking'' with him.

"Let me rephrase that,'' he said, obviously fighting a smile as his end-of-flight tasks came to a conclusion and he turned toward her. ''The B and B is the only thing we have in the way of a hotel or motel so there isn't really a choice but to stay with me. But you won't actually be staying *with* me. My cabin has an attic room complete with its own bathroom, and it can only be reached by an outside staircase. So in actuality it's a separate residence. Well, except that you'll need to use my kitchen. But it's a pretty cozy room that I'm sure you'll be comfortable in. And I promise you'll have complete privacy.''

Again Emmy was reminded of her predecessor and of Evelyn's gripes about some of the accommodations she'd had to suffer through. And even if the attic room of Aiden Tarlington's cabin was nice enough, there was the added complication of being in close proximity to the man and how awkward that might be. Emmy didn't appreciate this situation any more than Evelyn would have. Plus she knew it would only be made worse if she didn't find a way to curb her heightened awareness of how attractive he was.

"There's *nowhere* else I could stay?'' she asked.

"Sorry.''

Emmy chewed that over in her mind to get used to it.

Certainly it would have been preferable to stay somewhere else. Away from him and the odd effect he seemed to have on her. But if that wasn't an option it wasn't an option, and she'd have to make the best of the situation.

Besides, she assured herself, before too long she would get used to being around him and stop even noticing how attractive he was. This whole situation—and his knock-'em-dead good looks—were all just a novelty. A novelty that would wear off.

And as soon as it did, there wouldn't be a problem.

She hoped.

Aiden's cabin was made of rough-hewn logs and was situated near an evergreen-bordered lake with nothing else as far as the eye could see around it.

Moonlight reflected on the undisturbed, glassy surface of the water to cast the only light as Aiden took her bags onto the front porch. He bypassed the door to the lower level and instead went around to the right side of the building.

Emmy followed, finding a wooden staircase there.

"Let's get your things upstairs and turn on the space heater to warm the place while we have a little something to eat."

Emmy was all for warmth, because he hadn't been exaggerating about the cold that was even more noticeable here than it had been in Fairbanks.

The second floor was one large room except for the

bathroom. One large room with a brass bed, an over-stuffed chair, a reading lamp and a very old armoire. And nothing else.

Emmy thought that *cozy* was stretching the truth a bit, but she didn't say that.

"The bed has a feather mattress," Aiden informed her as he set her suitcases on the wooden floor that hadn't seen stain or varnish in several decades. "I hope you aren't allergic."

"I'm not," she said as she poked her head into the bathroom, where she found toilet, sink and a claw-footed bathtub with a very dated showerhead dropping down from directly over the middle of the tub.

Aiden had turned on the space heater by the time she returned from inspecting the bathroom.

"I wouldn't recommend using the heater all night long. It can get pretty hot if it's on for hours at a time. And there's an electric blanket on the bed, under the quilt, so you'll be warm enough while you sleep. Getting out of bed in the morning is just sort of a shock to the system."

"I can imagine."

"Wakes you up, though."

"Mmm."

"Come on, let's go downstairs. I have some sandwiches made up since we didn't have any in-flight food service."

He held the door open for her, and Emmy went out into the cold again.

At the bottom of the steps Aiden went ahead of her to the main door. As he did, her gaze dropped inadvertently to the jeans-clad derriere that was visible below his jacket.

Like the rest of him it was something to behold, and Emmy silently chastised herself for looking, snapping her eyes up to a safer view.

But the view wasn't actually much safer when she took in the expanse of his back and broad, broad shoulders, or the sexy way his hair waved against his thick, strong neck.

"Ladies first," he said then, and she noticed belatedly that he was waiting for her to go in ahead of him.

Emmy stepped into the cabin, glad for the warmth coming from the old radiator against one wall.

The place seemed about double the size of the attic room but it still wasn't large. Or luxurious. Living room, dining room and kitchen were all one open space, with a mud room off the kitchen in the rear and a single bedroom and another bath on the other side of a log-framed archway to the left of the living room.

The furnishings were as inelegant as the cabin itself. There was a brown plaid sofa and matching easy chair at a ninety-degree angle to each other, with a wagon wheel coffee table in front of them and a moderately sized television and VCR across from them.

Aiden's stereo equipment was on an arrangement of stacked cinder blocks against one wall, there was a fairly nice desk taking up another, and a scarred oak kitchen table and four ladder-backed chairs stood in what passed as a dining room only because the table and chairs were near the bar that separated the kitchen from the rest of the cabin.

"I know it's nothing fancy," Aiden said in response to Emmy's glance around. "But Boonesbury provides the cabin and most of the furniture for the local doctor, and I'm usually not here enough for it to matter that it isn't too aesthetically pleasing."

"But it is cozy," she said, mimicking him to tease him a little.

He laughed and she liked the sound of it. Along with the fact that he'd caught the joke.

He hadn't been kidding about already having sandwiches made. There was a covered plate of them in the refrigerator. He brought that and a bowl of potato salad along with two glasses of water to the kitchen table where they shared the light repast while Aiden filled her in on the quirks of the plumbing system and the party-line inconveniences she would encounter if she used any telephone in Boonesbury.

They'd finished eating and Aiden was on his way back to the fridge with the remaining sandwiches when there was a firm knock on the front door.

By then it was after ten o'clock and a drop-in visitor struck Emmy as strange.

But Aiden took it in stride and said over his shoulder, "Get that, will you?"

She'd already figured out that he was a very laid-back guy and that there weren't going to be any formalities even for the director of the Bernsdorf Foundation. So, in an attempt to adjust to the casual attitudes, she went to the door and opened it.

There was no one at eye level, but down below, on the porch floor, there was a baby carrier and a duffle bag.

Thinking that this couldn't possibly be what it looked like, Emmy stepped out into the cold to investigate.

But it was exactly what it looked like.

Amidst a nest of blankets and a hooded snowsuit there was a baby bundled into the car seat. A baby with two great big brown eyes staring up at her from over the pacifier that was keeping it quiet.

"I think you better come see this," she called to Aiden as she glanced all around and found no signs of anyone else.

But about the time Aiden came out onto the porch there was the sound of a vehicle racing away in the distance.

"What's going on?" Aiden asked.

"Good question. All I know is when I opened the door this was what I found—a duffle bag and a baby in a car seat. And I just heard a car or truck drive off."

"Oh-oh," Aiden said. But he didn't sound as unnerved as Emmy felt.

He went down off the porch, searching both sides of the cabin. But after only a minute or so he rejoined her, shrugging those mountain-man shoulders of his as he did.

"There's nobody out there anymore. But we'd better get this little guy—or girl—in out of the cold."

He picked up the carrier and the duffle bag and took them inside.

Emmy followed him all the way to the kitchen table, where he deposited everything, unbundled the baby and lifted it out.

"Hello, there." He greeted the child in a soothing voice he probably used with his youngest patients.

Then, to Emmy, he said, "Check the bag, see if there's a note or something that tells us who this is."

Emmy did as she was told, wondering if her predecessor had ever had a trip quite like this one was already turning out to be.

Along with baby clothes, diapers and food, she did find a note, albeit not much of one. Written on it was only one word: Mickey.

"Mickey, huh? Well, let's check you out a little, shall we, Mickey?" Aiden said when Emmy let him know what she'd found.

She watched as he took the baby to the sofa and laid it down there to unfasten the snowsuit. Then he removed the pajamas that were underneath it, and then the diaper.

"Looks like Mickey is a boy," Aiden announced unnecessarily, replacing the diaper in a hurry and with more expertise than Emmy would have had. "Don't let him roll off the sofa," he instructed, going for his medical bag where he'd left it on a table near the front door.

Bringing it back with him, he went on to examine the child who was still watching everything with wide eyes and sucking on the pacifier, only protesting when

Aiden used the stethoscope to listen to his heart and lungs.

"I'd say Mickey, here, is about seven months old, well fed and taken care of and as healthy as they come," was the final diagnosis.

"And why was he left on the porch? Or do you often have people drop off their children late at night for a checkup?"

"No, this is a first."

"You don't know the child or who he belongs to or where he came from?" Emmy asked with undisguised disbelief.

"I know as much as you do," Aiden said patiently.

Emmy stared at him, wondering how he could possibly be so calm about this.

Then something clicked in her brain and she began to replay all that had happened since she'd landed in Alaska. The need to take the small plane into the middle of nowhere. To stay in a strange, distractingly attractive man's cabin away from everything and everyone, in a room without central heat. And now a baby left on the doorstep?

This had to be some kind of practical joke Howard was playing on her.

Or maybe it was a test to see how she handled whatever curves came her way and to find out if she really was better suited to the job than Evelyn had been.

"This is all a setup, right?" she heard herself say. "Howard just wants to see how I deal with the unexpected, if I can keep my eye on the ball and not get overly involved in matters that don't concern me. I know he thought Evelyn didn't make it as director because she was so freaked out by the things that happened on these trips. He thought that she took everything too seriously and too personally, that she got too involved in things that didn't have anything to do with the grants, that she lost sight of what she was in these communities to do, of what was and what wasn't her business and let the wrong things influence her recommendations. So he decided to put me through trial by fire, didn't he?''

Aiden settled Mickey on his knee and looked at Emmy as if she'd lost her mind. "The only thing Howard set up was the opportunity for Boonesbury to be considered for the grant.''

"Come on. Making me fly in the same kind of plane Evelyn nearly crashed in? Making me stay here? A baby left on the porch the minute I arrive? Howard arranged it all.''

"I'm sorry, Emmy, but he didn't. This is just the way things are.''

It was not a good sign that even in the middle of this the sound of him saying her name made her melt a little inside, and she wondered if she was just on some kind of overload. She had been up since four o'clock that morning, after all, and it had hardly been a relaxing day.

But still she didn't give up the notion that Howard had planned what had happened since she'd landed in Alaska to test her. And she knew that even if he had, his cohort here wasn't likely to confess from the get-go.

"Okay, fine. This is just the way things are," Emmy repeated with a note of facetiousness. "So what does that mean? That while I'm here and you're giving me the tour of Boonesbury's medical needs we're going to deal with an abandoned baby, too?"

"Well, it looks like I am. I don't have a choice. Somebody left this baby here, and they must have had a reason. For now I need to find out who that person is and what the reason was and decide what to do about it. But I won't let it—or Mickey—stand in the way of what you're here to do. Boonesbury really could benefit from that grant money."

"And you're just going to take it in stride," Emmy said, still finding it difficult to believe anyone could be so cool about it all.

Aiden Tarlington shrugged his shoulders again. "This is Alaska. Things in Fairbanks, Anchorage, Juneau—the cities—are pretty much what you'd find in the lower forty-eight. But out here there's a mix of stubborn independence and neighbor helping neighbor. I know these people and I know this baby being here could mean just about anything. But, like I said, I'll make sure it doesn't interfere with what you're here to do, or impact on you in any way."

And if this was all some kind of test Howard had set up, she decided on the spot that she was going to pass it. That she wasn't going to get upset by this turn of events and call the head of the board of trustees to whine about it the way Evelyn would have. That she wasn't going to take it upon herself to care for that baby even if she was itching to hold him and comfort him and let him know he was with people who would be kind to him. That she wasn't going to let herself be distracted the way Evelyn would have been. Or let herself be swayed in Boonesbury's favor because she was already having her heartstrings tugged.

She was there to assess medical needs of the entire area and community and that was all. Period. Finito. That was the total sum and substance of what she was concerning herself with. She knew that Howard had very nearly not given her the job because Evelyn had left him with so many doubts that a woman could do it. Doubts that a woman could weather the hardships of these trips and remain objective in the face of the things she might see. And Emmy was going to prove him wrong.

So, with all of that in mind, Emmy tried to ignore Mickey by raising her chin and her gaze high enough not to see him and said, "I'm sure everything will work out. But if you don't mind, I've had a really long day and I think I'll leave you to do whatever you need to with Mickey to get him settled in for the night."

"Sure. You must be beat. There won't be any rush to get out of here tomorrow, so you can sleep in as long as you want and we'll just go into town whenever you're ready."

"Great."

Aiden stood to walk her to the door, taking Mickey

along with him. "If you need anything just stomp on the floor a couple of times and I'll come running."

"Okay. Good luck with this," Emmy added, nodding at Mickey.

"Thanks," Aiden said with a small chuckle, as if he could use some luck.

Or a benefactor who hadn't enlisted him to test the new director, Emmy thought. Although she was impressed by how good he was at the charade. Obviously, Howard had chosen well in his coconspirator.

Emmy opened the front door and flinched at the blast of cold air that came in. "Better keep Mickey out of the draft," she advised. "I'll close this behind me."

Aiden nodded, staying a few feet back.

"Good night," Emmy said.

"Sleep well."

She pushed open the screen door, then stepped out onto the porch and turned to pull the wooden door shut.

But as she did she couldn't help taking one last look at Aiden Tarlington, standing there holding that baby, and she was struck by what an appealing sight it was to see the big, muscular man cradling the infant in his arms.

But she wasn't going to let any of it get to her, she reminded herself firmly.

Not the adorable, abandoned baby.

Not the wilderness.

Not the rustic room without heat.

Not the idea of needing to fly back to civilization in the tiny plane when this was over.

And not the drop-dead-gorgeous, sexy doctor she was sort of living with.

Evelyn, Emmy knew, would never have been able to keep her mind on the job with all these distractions.

But Emmy was determined that she would.

Chapter Two

Aiden woke up early the next morning and immediately rolled to his side to peer down at his youngest
houseguest.

He'd pumped up an air mattress and placed it between the bed and the wall as a makeshift crib, but
he hadn't been sure it was the safest way for the baby
to sleep. Worrying about it had made for a restless
night. But, as he had on every other bed check, he
found Mickey sound asleep, peacefully making sucking noises as if he were practicing for breakfast.

Even though it came as a relief to see once again
that the infant was all right, Aiden didn't hold out
much hope of falling back to sleep himself. The sun
wasn't anywhere near rising yet, so he rolled to his
back again, closed his eyes and tried to relax enough
to maybe doze off.

Except that now he could hear those sucking sounds and he just kept thinking, What the hell am I doing with a baby...?

He'd thought he'd pretty much seen it all up here during the past seven years. But he had to admit that having a baby left on his doorstep was a new one. He delivered babies, he didn't have them left with him.

As he'd put his tiny charge to bed he'd tried to figure out if Mickey was one of the babies he'd delivered seven months or so ago, but he hadn't been able to tell. A newborn and a seven-month-old didn't look much alike. Even the eye color often changed. And it wasn't as if he could remember specific, identifying features of each baby, because he couldn't.

And then there was the other possibility. The possibility he didn't want to consider. The possibility he had to consider even if he didn't want to.

What if Mickey was his? What if that was the reason he'd been left with him?

If it hadn't been for one single night, he would have been able to say there was no way that it was possible that he was Mickey's father. But there had been that one single night. And when he'd counted backward—seven months for what he guessed to be Mickey's age and then another nine months gestation—he had to admit that that one single night could have, in fact, resulted in Mickey.

That thought chased sleep further from his grasp, and Aiden opened his eyes to stare at the ceiling.

One single night...

One single night when his marriage had fallen

apart, when Rebecca had left him, that he'd gone into town and drowned his sorrow in a whiskey bottle.

And ended up sleeping with Nora Finley.

But until now he'd thought sleeping was all they'd done.

Even now he couldn't remember anything beyond being in Boonesbury's bar to tie one on and meeting up with Nora.

He only knew that when he finally came to the next morning, there had been a note on the pillow beside him that said, "Thanks for a good time, Nora."

But since he'd still had his pants on he'd assumed the "good time" they'd had had merely been drinks and laughs and maybe sharing a platonic mattress.

He'd been sure that nothing else had happened. He liked Nora well enough but she was a long—*long*—way from his type. To say she was rough around the edges was a kind description of the woman who had hacked out a place in the woods to build her cabin with her own two hands, and who made her living running dogsled races. And rough around the edges was not something he'd ever found attractive.

But now he couldn't be absolutely positive that nothing beyond drinks and laughs had happened. Maybe he *had* offered her more than a place to crash for a night.

Mickey didn't look like Nora, Aiden reminded himself, in an effort to find something to hang some hope on to. Mickey didn't look like Aiden, either. Or like anyone Aiden knew.

But the hope he derived from that was fleeting. Looks were hardly conclusive proof of anything.

Which meant that he was going to have to do some investigating. Some testing. Some questioning.

And all right away.

Unfortunately.

Because although this was not something he ever wanted to be faced with, having it happen now was phenomenally bad timing.

He was grateful to Howard Wilson for submitting Boonesbury for the grant that Emmy Harris was there to consider them for. The money would be a huge help in updating the care he could give, and Aiden had planned to do everything he could to convince her to recommend that they get it. Only now he had Mickey and this whole situation to deal with, too.

But there was nothing he could do about it. He just had to hope that Emmy Harris would be as understanding and patient as she was lovely to look at.

That thought made him nervous the moment after he'd had it. On two counts.

First of all, Emmy Harris had already *not* seemed patient and understanding about Mickey. Actually Mickey's arrival had sort of pushed her over the edge, Aiden recalled, as he considered the end of last evening and the foundation's director saying what she'd said about Howard setting up these complications, about this being a trial by fire.

She hadn't seemed patient or understanding then. She'd seemed agitated.

And second of all, what was he doing thinking about her being lovely?

That didn't have a place in any of this.

It was tough to ignore, though, he secretly admitted to himself.

Because she really was a knockout. And a whole lot more his type than Nora Finley.

Not that he was interested in Emmy Harris personally. But, purely on an empirical basis, she was a very attractive woman. How could he not notice that? How could he not notice that she had skin as flawless as Mickey's? And high cheekbones that no plastic surgeon could have fashioned as well? And a small nose with the faintest hint of a bump on the bridge that kept it from being too perfect and ended up making it just plain cute? And lips full enough to inspire images of long, slow kisses...

Fast—think about what you didn't like about her, he ordered himself before his mind ventured too much farther afield than it already had.

He hadn't been wild about that bun her hair had been in—that was something he hadn't liked.

Although the hair itself was a great color—rich mink-brown all shot through with russet red.

And her eyes were a fascinating color, too. Dark brown but with rays of glittering green all through them so that first he'd thought they were brown and then he'd wondered if they were green, before he'd finally sat across the kitchen table from her and been able to really figure it out.

Plus there were those legs of hers. Terrific legs.

Any woman in a skirt and nylons was a rare, bordering-on-nonexistent sight in Boonesbury. But even if it had been an everyday occurrence, her legs would have caught his attention. Long, shapely legs that made them a particular treat.

A treat that only started there. It continued all the way up a great little body that was just curvy enough to let him know she was a woman underneath that stuffy suit and high-collared blouse.

Oh, yeah, she was easy on the eyes.

And smart.

And she had a sense of humor, too—something he was really a sucker for in a woman....

Aiden mentally yanked himself up short when he again realized the direction his thoughts had wandered.

So much for thinking about what he *didn't* like about her.

But even when he tried to come up with something else, he couldn't. The bun was about it in the negatives column. And he had no doubt one swipe of a hairbrush would take care of that.

Which was probably why, even in spite of the mess with Mickey, he was looking forward to this next week more than he had been before he'd met Emmy Harris.

This isn't a social event, he reminded himself.

This week was work. And that was the only way he should be thinking about it.

Besides, even if Emmy Harris had been there for

some other reason, Aiden knew better than to let down his guard with a woman like her.

She might be more his type than Nora Finley, but he could tell the minute she'd stepped up to him at the airport that she was not the kind of person who could make a go of life in the Alaskan wilderness.

Emmy Harris might *look* pretty special, but he knew right off the bat that she wasn't the kind of special to live where high fashion translated to anorak jackets, mukluks and thermal underwear. Where the only restaurant was also the gas station and the mayor's office. Where there wasn't a shopping mall within driving distance. Where a fair share of women—like Nora—considered cutting their nails with a gutting knife to be a manicure.

And if there was one thing Aiden already knew from painful experience it was that it was a losing battle to make any attempt to fit the round-peg kind of woman Emmy Harris was into the square hole of Boonesbury.

Oh, no, that wasn't something he'd ever try again.

But even so, he thought as the sun began to make its first appearance through the open curtains of his bedroom window, he did have to admit that having the foundation's beautiful director there with him for a little while would be a nice change of pace.

Of course it would have been a nicer change of pace if he didn't have an abandoned baby and possible fatherhood looming over his head at the same time to distract him, but it was still a nice change of pace, anyway.

On the other hand, considering how intensely aware he'd been of every detail about Emmy just in the first few hours of knowing her, maybe having Mickey around as a buffer was a good thing.

Mickey made a noise just then that sounded different from the sucking noises, and Aiden rolled to his side again to check on him.

When he did he found the baby's eyes open and his fist in his mouth.

Mickey left the fist where it was but looked up at Aiden with curiosity.

"Morning, little guy," he said softly.

Mickey granted him a tentative smile from behind the fist.

"Ready to get up?" Aiden asked as if the infant would answer him.

Mickey grinned even bigger, as if that idea had thrilled him.

"Okay, but here's what I'm thinking," Aiden informed the baby. "I'll get you cleaned up and fed, and then you're going to have to pay me back by keeping things on the up and up while Ms. Emmy Harris is around. You can't let me do anything stupid. What do you say?"

Mickey finally removed his fist from his mouth and blew a spit bubble for him.

"I'll take that as a yes."

But Aiden was worried that Mickey had his work cut out for him.

Because as he got out of bed to pick up the baby

he could feel the itch to see Emmy again, to hear her voice, to catch a whiff of her perfume.

An itch so strong he wasn't sure how he was going to ignore it.

Even if the medical future of the whole county was riding on it.

For Emmy there was ordinarily nothing like a good night's sleep to recharge her batteries and help her face the day.

But she had had nothing like a good night's sleep. And when she woke up at five minutes after seven, she was aggravated with herself. Even if she was on a business trip, it was Sunday and there was no hurry getting to work. The least her body could have done was to have let her get some rest.

Although, it wasn't actually her body at fault. Her body was supremely comfortable in the feather bed.

It was her mind that had kept her awake most of the night. Her mind that had kicked up again now.

She kept her eyes closed and took deep breaths, willing herself not to think about anything.

Just sleep, she told herself. Just sleep...

But her nose was so cold where it poked above the covers that she thought that might be keeping her awake.

Which meant she would have to get up, have her bare feet touch an undoubtedly frigid floor, expose herself completely to what her nose was suffering already and go all the way to the far corner of the room to turn on the space heater.

What exactly was it that people saw in rustic living? It was a mystery to her.

She sighed and resigned herself to having to leave her warm cocoon to get some heat in the place.

Flinging aside the electric blanket and quilt, she ran on tiptoes to the space heater to turn it on, then dived back under the covers again.

But that mad dash didn't save her, and even after she was back in the warm bed a chill shook her whole body like a leaf in the wind.

How could any place in the twenty-first century—especially in Alaska—not have central heat, for crying out loud?

But once the chill had passed and the room was beginning to warm up, Emmy relaxed again and admitted that it was nice under that electric blanket and the weight of the quilt. She even began to wonder if maybe she'd be able to fall asleep again after all.

She closed her eyes and gave it a try.

Just sleep. Just sleep...

But would her stubborn brain give her a break?

Absolutely not.

It started spinning with the same thoughts that had kept her up most of the night—that it was a dirty trick Howard was playing on her to put all these obstacles in her way to test her on her very first trip for the foundation.

But he wasn't going to get the best of her. The determination to pass the test was stronger this morning than it had been the night before.

She figured that she'd already overcome some of the obstacles: she'd gotten on that small plane rather than allowing fear to rule; she'd left Aiden Tarlington to contend with the baby rather than digging in as if it were her problem; and she'd made it through her first night in the attic room without heat.

So there, Howard!

Of course, she'd also spent the night tormented with vivid images of Aiden Tarlington and a strange longing to be back downstairs with him.

But that didn't count as a failure of the test; keeping her from sleeping was not foundation business. It only counted as foundation business if she was distracted from her reason for being here. And while the much-too-attractive doctor had the potential to do just that, she was not going to let it happen.

Any more than she was going to let herself get sidetracked by the complications of the oh-so-cute baby who had come onto the scene last night.

Because although it might not be easy to keep her focus, she was going to do it. She really was. Howard was not going to win this one.

She'd fought for this job, and now that she had it, she was going to do it. She was going to do it better than anyone had ever done it before her—man or woman. And without a peep of complaint.

She just needed to wear blinders of a sort. She needed to block out the effects of Aiden Tarlington's appeal, the draw of the adorable Mickey, and keep her eye on the ball.

And that was what she was going to do.

The little pep talk bolstered her confidence and she felt herself actually beginning to drift off to sleep again.

And if while she did, the picture of Aiden Tarlington came back into her mind and made something warm and fuzzy inside her stir to life?

Well, she wasn't working at the moment, was she?

There may have been no hurry for Emmy to join Aiden for the tour of Boonesbury but, when the next time her eyes opened it was eleven o'clock, she bolted out of bed in a panic. What kind of impression did it make for the foundation's director to sleep that late?

She rushed to the bathroom to take a shower but that was no quick thing. She had to deal with the peculiarities of a pitifully poor spray of water that literally ran hot one minute, cold the next, and never just warm enough to stand under.

She'd wanted to do something nice with her hair. Something nicer, more youthful and definitely more attractive than the bun. But that would have taken too long so she ended up leaving it to fall loosely around her shoulders.

And as for clothes, she could hardly dawdle when it came to deciding what to wear, and quickly chose a pair of black slacks and a long-sleeved, white, split-V-neck T-shirt. Then she applied blush and mascara—as fast as she did in her car on the way to her office when she'd slept through her alarm.

Yet it was still noon before she grabbed the black knee-length cardigan sweater she'd brought with her and bounded down the stairs to knock on Aiden's door.

"It's open. Come on in."

A shiver that had nothing to do with the barely above-freezing temperature outside actually shook her at the sound of his voice through the closed door. Before she opened it she reminded herself how much she had riding on this trip and how much damage she could do to herself by allowing an unprofessional response to this man.

Besides, she'd already had her life scrambled by a nature boy, and she knew better than to get too close to another one. She and Aiden Tarlington were oil and water, and the two just didn't mix.

Remember that, she ordered herself as she went inside.

"Hi," he greeted, the moment she did.

He was sitting at the kitchen table with Mickey in the baby carrier in front of him so that he could feed the infant what looked to be applesauce.

Emmy returned his greeting and then debated about making an excuse for why she was putting in such a late appearance. But the fact that Aiden didn't question her gave her the opportunity not to explain herself and so she didn't.

"We're just finishing up lunch here," he informed her. "Help yourself to something to eat."

Emmy was struck all over again by the lack of formality, but she went to the other side of the counter and poured herself a cup of coffee.

There were still a few sandwiches from the night

before in the fridge and, in the interest of letting him think she'd been up for more than an hour, she chose one of those to bring back with her to the table rather than having the toast or cereal she would have preferred as her first meal of the day.

As Emmy joined Aiden and Mickey at the table, Aiden was intent on persuading the baby to accept another bite of food. Not being in the conversation left Emmy free to drink in the sight of the big man.

He had on blue jeans and a blue-plaid flannel shirt with the sleeves rolled to his elbows exposing the cuffs of a darker blue crew-neck T-shirt that also showed behind the open collar. He looked more like a lumberjack than a doctor but he was something to behold nevertheless.

"So I see Mickey is still here," Emmy commented, when the infant took the spoonful of what was indeed applesauce.

"Still here," Aiden confirmed.

"Mmm-hmm. And you're still going with the story that he was just left here," Emmy said, unable to suppress a knowing smile at what she was convinced was an elaborate ruse instigated by Howard.

"I'm still going with the story because it's the only story there is."

She decided to call his bluff. "If Mickey has really been abandoned shouldn't you call the police or Child Protective Services or someone with the authority to do something about it?"

Aiden showed no sign of wavering. "That might be what I should do if I was somewhere else," he explained smoothly. "But we don't have anyone in Boonesbury to call. State police provide law enforcement on the rare occasions we need it, but since this isn't an emergency it could be days or even weeks before they get around to sending someone. There's a Social Services office in Fairbanks but I'd have to take Mickey to them."

"That seems like what you should do, then," Emmy said, still testing.

Until something else even more outlandish occurred to her.

"Unless he could be yours," she said with a full measure of challenge in her tone.

But Aiden didn't pick up the gauntlet she'd dropped. He didn't raise his eyebrows at the very suggestion. He didn't balk and defend himself in instant outrage.

Instead his slightly bushy eyebrows pulled into a frown that actually seemed unnerved by exactly that possibility.

"*Could* he be yours?" Emmy repeated in shock.

Again there was no quick denial.

In his own sweet time Aiden said, "I'm going to have to do some digging before I can answer that."

Which obviously meant that there was a possibility Mickey might be his.

And for absolutely no reason Emmy could put her finger on, she felt a swell of something that seemed like jealousy. Although, of course that couldn't have been what it was.

"Oh," she said quietly, hating that she sounded so incredulous.

Aiden didn't seem to notice, though. He was very serious now and he stopped feeding Mickey to level those incredible blue eyes on her. "I know it looks bad that there's even the chance that I could have a baby I had no idea existed. You're probably thinking it makes me an irresponsible jerk who shouldn't be caring for Boonesbury's citizens, let alone be the person who would oversee your grant money. But it isn't like that."

Actually she'd been too stunned to think anything. But she let silence pretend that was exactly what had been on her mind so he would go on.

Which was what he did.

"It's a long, personal story," he said. "But *if* Mickey is mine—and I'm not convinced that he is—but *if* he is, it was a matter of one night when I hit rock bottom and pickled myself in a bottle of scotch. Now that's something I'd never done before and haven't done since. But that night I ended up so out of it I don't remember what happened. Until now I'd been sure nothing had, and that may still be the case. Mickey's being left here could be something entirely separate from that night. From me. I just don't know. But either way, I'll have to find out what's going on."

Emmy stared at him. Intently. She searched his eyes, his handsome face. And she suddenly began to doubt that this was a test Howard had set up. This man was too uncomfortable admitting this to her, too embarrassed to *have* to admit it to her, for it not to be real.

"Did you call the woman who could be Mickey's mother to ask if he's yours?" Emmy inquired, maybe testing just a little more.

"The woman's name is Nora Finley and I haven't seen or heard from her since that night I thought I'd just given her a place to stay. She lives in a cabin a long way from anywhere and she doesn't have a phone. She'll have to be tracked down, and the best way to do that is to put out a message over the radio. There's a station in Cochran—that's the nearest town to Boonesbury. Their signal is strong so it gets picked up pretty far out. I called there and they're going to report on Mickey on their newscast, requesting that anyone with any information about him contact me or the station, and they'll be broadcasting regular messages from me to Nora, asking for Nora to contact me as soon as possible. That will all start tomorrow since they don't air on Sunday."

So he was trying to reach this woman over public airwaves to ask if they'd slept together, if she'd had his baby and if she'd left that baby on his doorstep?

No one would choose to do that unless they had to.

"This isn't something Howard arranged in order to see how I handled complications and distractions on these trips, is it?"

Aiden shook his head. "I wish that's all this was. But it isn't. I told you that."

"Someone actually packed up their child and brought him to you without warning or explanation."

"I'm afraid that's how it looks."

"And it's a coincidence that it happened now?"

"A lousy coincidence that I'm trying to make the best of."

Maybe she was letting down her guard, but she believed him. It was all just too crazy to be invented, and in the light of day, looking at Aiden's expression, she honestly didn't think anyone could be that adept an actor.

"Okay, I'm going to give you the benefit of the doubt," she finally said. "But if this is all something you and Howard devised—"

"Why would I risk all of Boonesbury's medical future?" Aiden cut her off to ask. "I know your recommendation makes or breaks that grant. Even with Howard's endorsement there are still six other votes that have to go Boonesbury's way in order to get the money. If you go back and tell them not to give it to us, Howard's one vote in our favor isn't going to amount to a hill of beans."

That was all true and swayed Emmy more in the direction of letting go of her assumption that Howard had arranged a trial by fire for her. Apparently Evelyn's complaints that these trips rarely went smoothly had some merit.

But that was all right, Emmy consoled herself. She was good at multitasking and she'd put that into play here.

"Then I guess we'll just deal with this along the way," she finally said.

Mickey, who had lost interest in his applesauce and instead had turned his attention to Emmy, cooed at her as if he were giving his approval.

And Emmy, who had been trying not to notice how cute he was, finally gave in and laughed at him. "You like that idea, do you?" she asked the baby.

Mickey giggled as a reward.

"Does this mean you'll do diaper duty?" Aiden asked, sounding relieved and relaxed again.

"Oh, no. There has to be a line drawn," Emmy joked in response to the note of teasing in his tone. "The only diapers I'm signing on for are for kids of my own if I ever have any."

"Guess I'll have to take care of it, then, so we can get going. Will you keep an eye on him while I clear away his lunch?"

"That I'll do," Emmy agreed.

She was finished with her sandwich, so when Aiden got up from the chair in front of Mickey she replaced him.

The seat was still warm from his body, and of all the things to find sexy she didn't think that should be one of them.

But that's how it was just the same and it left her fighting images of his body wrapped all around her.

Luckily Mickey seemed to have made it his goal to entertain and charm her because he helped get her mind off the image by drawing her attention back to him with enthusiastic waves of his arms and kicks of his legs.

Only too willing to comply, Emmy grasped his feet in her hands and made a bicycle motion that delighted him as she studied him.

He was an absolutely adorable baby with those big brown eyes and those chubby cheeks. He had pale-brown hair that cupped his round head like feathers and two tiny teeth just beginning to poke through the center of his bottom gums.

"How could anybody leave you on a stranger's doorstep?" she asked in a cooing sort of way that belied the words.

Mickey apparently responded to the tone rather than the content because he grinned at her and made a grab for her hair.

"That'll hurt if you let him do it," Aiden advised as he rejoined them.

"Oh, I think I could stand it," Emmy said in a singsong as she rubbed Mickey's knees with her nose to make him laugh.

"Don't be too sure."

Aiden had laid a towel on the counter that separated the kitchen from the rest of the cabin, and he took Mickey out of the car seat then to lay him on the towel to change him and get him into his snow-suit.

As he did, Emmy finished her coffee and washed her cup to replace it in the cupboard. Then, after Aiden had bundled the baby back into the carrier the way Mickey had been the previous night when they'd found him, Aiden put on that same jean jacket he'd worn the day before, tossed a few diapers, the pacifier and a bottle in a plastic bag to take with them, and carried the car seat outside to the SUV. With Emmy following behind.

"Why don't you start the engine so it'll warm up while I figure out how to strap this thing in the back seat?"

Again, no standing on ceremony.

But Emmy was getting used to the fact that things between them were so casual and she didn't mind it. She was even beginning to like it a little.

"Okay," she agreed, catching the keys Aiden tossed to her with an ease that seemed to impress him.

Emmy was waiting in the passenger seat and the engine was warm enough to produce heat before Aiden finally judged the carrier secure and slipped behind the wheel.

"I talked to Joan—the woman who owns the local store," he said as he put the SUV into gear and pulled away from the cabin. "She's meeting us at one-thirty so we can get the shopping over with before I show you around town. I didn't think you should be doing a lot of walking until we got you a coat."

"Okay."

Something about that made him smile a smile that might have been a smirk on a less handsome face. "What? No more of the 'I'm not susceptible to the cold' stuff?"

"I'm conceding to your greater experience in the

tundra," she said as if she were merely humoring him.

"This is nothing compared to the tundra," he said with a laugh. "But if you want to sneak a peek at that—"

"No, thanks. Boonesbury and the complete tour of the medical needs it serves will be fine."

"In a warm coat," he goaded. But his grin was every bit as infectious and charming as Mickey's, only with a whole lot more grown-up appeal.

He went on looking at her out of the corner of his eye for a moment longer. Then he said, "I like your hair down better than in that librarian bun, by the way. The bun doesn't suit you."

"It has its purpose."

"Probably to make sure Howard and the rest of the Old Boys take you seriously."

Emmy's expression must have shown her surprise—both at his correct assumption of the reason she wore the bun and at the term *Old Boys*.

As if Aiden knew what she was thinking even now, he said, "Yeah, they know you call them the Old Boys, so don't ever say it without affection."

"Howard told you that?"

"It came up. But since he's the youngest of the trustees he figures you're referring to everyone but him."

"Great," Emmy muttered to herself facetiously.

"There's no offense taken, so don't worry about it."

The two-lane road they were on went over a ridge

just then and began a steep decline that brought
Boonesbury into view. It changed the subject as Aiden nodded with his chin in that direction.

"There she is—the town of Boonesbury."

To call what Emmy was looking at a town seemed
like an exaggeration.

It reminded her of the old frontier in Western movies. There was a single main street not more than four
blocks long and so wide it was as if the buildings on
one side were trying to keep their distance from the
buildings on the other. What few cars and trucks were
parked in front of the peeling-paint one- and two-
story structures were aimed nosefirst to the curb and
even then there was room for three regular-width
lanes in between.

From the vantage point of the hill she could see
houses all around what passed for Boonesbury's thor-
oughfare, scattered as erratically as marbles tossed on
the ground. Some of them were close enough together
to be considered neighborhoods of sorts, others sat
off alone as if anyone who had been inclined had
staked out a plot of ground for themselves.

And that was it.

Which was exactly what Emmy said. "That's it?"

"That's the heart of the town. The business district,
I suppose you could call it. There's more—a lot
more—that's Boonesbury county, it's just too wide-
spread to see from any one spot."

As they drove into town, Aiden pointed out the
highlights of the businesses they passed.

They were all small businesses—no chain stores or

recognizable names were anywhere to be seen—and only the bare necessities of the community seemed to be served.

There was a barber shop and a beauty shop side by side in the same building. An accountant and a lawyer shared an office. There was a mechanic. A tiny bank. An equally as tiny chapel for a church. An insurance office. And several other places that offered more than one interest per establishment—the Laundromat was also the library, the snowblower sales and repair shop was also the post office, the local mortician also sold real estate and acted as travel agent, and, as Aiden had said before, the only restaurant was also the mayor's office and the gas station.

The general store was housed in the largest building, a white clapboard structure two levels high with a recessed front door and cantilevered display windows on either side of it.

Aiden parked in front, and once he'd taken the baby carrier out of the back seat they were let into the store by a tall woman with an extremely long nose and kind green eyes.

Aiden introduced her as Joan, and as Emmy went to explore the shop that carried everything from groceries to underwear to farm equipment, she could hear him telling the other woman about Mickey, asking if she recognized the baby or knew anything about him.

Joan didn't, but before they left the store Emmy bought a down-filled parka, three sweaters, another pair of jeans and some warmer socks, and Aiden purchased a travel crib, more diapers, formula and baby food.

Introducing Emmy, showing off Mickey and telling his story, and asking about Nora Finley became a pattern once they'd left the store and begun their trek along the street. A number of the shops were closed, but there were still people milling around between the few that opened on Sunday, and since Aiden knew everyone they encountered, they all stopped to talk.

By midafternoon they'd gone completely up one side of the street and down the other with Aiden providing commentary about every building and most every owner and employee. Plus, Emmy had met more people than she'd ever be able to remember, and word of Mickey's situation was well spread.

Aiden suggested they get in out of the cold for a cup of coffee and they ended up at the Boonesbury Inn—the only restaurant and bar.

It was a big adobe building with water-stained walls and four wooden steps up to a scarred double door.

The place was packed with people sitting on stools at the bar to watch a baseball game on the television, playing pool on the three tables that occupied the rear or sitting at the tables and booths where food was being served.

Aiden and Emmy got the last booth, which was where they spent the remainder of the day doing as they'd done through the rest of the city tour with people they hadn't yet spoken to. But with no better results—no one recognized Mickey or knew anything about Nora Finley.

Through it all Emmy was struck by the friendliness of the whole town, though, and by the time they left the place—after coffee evolved into a dinner of hamburgers and fries and Mickey had been passed around like a football—Emmy was actually beginning to appreciate the warmth of Boonesbury.

Mickey was sound asleep when they got him home, and Emmy offered to get him ready for bed while Aiden set up the travel crib.

The baby slept through the change and went right on sleeping as Aiden set him in the crib that he'd put alongside his own bed—the bed that Emmy had to work very hard not to picture Aiden in when she brought Mickey into the bedroom.

And then Mickey was down for the night and Aiden was ushering her out of the room, and she knew she should say good-night and go up to her own room.

She just didn't know what she was going to do up there since it was only nine o'clock and there wasn't a television or a radio and she didn't feel like reading the book she'd brought along for the trip.

Aiden solved the problem by reminding her that the space heater needed to be turned on to warm the attic room in advance, leaving her to wait downstairs while he did it.

"How about a little brandy to chase away the chill?" he suggested when he returned.

Neither of them had had anything stronger to drink

than coffee and water at the inn, so a small drink now didn't seem so out of the question. Even if she was there on business, Emmy reasoned, there had to come a time when she was off the clock.

"Sounds good," she said.

"Sit down and I'll get it."

He'd motioned to the sofa and that was where Emmy sat, hugging one end with her hip.

When Aiden joined her with the brandy he sat on the chair where he was closer to her than he would have been at the other end of the couch.

He'd been clean shaven when Emmy had come downstairs that morning, but his beard was beginning to shadow his jaw now. It added to his rugged masculinity and made him resemble a burly lumberjack all the more. A very attractive burly lumberjack.

"We didn't learn much about Mickey or the woman you think might be his mother," Emmy said to get her mind off just how good he looked.

"No, we didn't. I thought if it was Nora who left him, someone might have seen her at least pass through town."

"So maybe Mickey isn't hers." Or yours either, was the unspoken finish to that.

"Maybe. But I can't rule it out all the same. She could have come here and left again without ever going near Boonesbury."

"What's your next plan of action? Or is it just to see if the radio announcements tomorrow bring any information?"

"The radio announcements only *start* tomorrow,

they'll go on until I stop them. But, no, I can't just leave it at that. I thought we'd spend tomorrow at the office. Monday is always a full day, and it'll give you a chance to see what goes on. Then, when I get a minute to spare, I'll take some of Mickey's blood to type it, see how it compares to mine. And to Nora's, if I have that in her file.''

Obviously, he hadn't ruled himself out as Mickey's father.

Thinking along that line, Emmy said, ''I suppose it is hard to understand why anyone would leave him with you if you're *not* his father.''

But her assumption that Aiden was leaning more in that direction was wrong.

''Actually, it isn't all that far-fetched. As the only doctor for miles, and one of the few people educated beyond high school, I hold a pretty unique position. Even folks who shy away from civilization or value their independence and self-reliance above all else, still come to me with their problems—medical and sometimes otherwise. Basically, they trust me around here.''

''In other words, if someone was going to leave their baby on another person's doorstep, you'd be the likeliest choice?''

''As a matter of fact.''

''That's an even heavier responsibility than most doctors have.''

''Maybe. But I like it that way. As I said, I'm not thrilled with having a baby left with me without any explanation—and in the middle of this grant stuff, to boot. But I like having a closer relationship with my patients. Knowing them by name. Knowing what's going on in their lives. Having them place that much confidence in me—''

''Having them leave you their babies...''

''I'd rather have that than have a cold, impersonal practice in a big city. If doing what I need to do with Mickey now and having to wonder if he's mine in the process are the trade-off for that, I'm okay with it.''

''And how about being bothered about sinus infections and migraines and foot fungus in a restaurant on a Sunday afternoon? Are you okay with that, too?'' Because that had been part of their afternoon as several people had used the opportunity of encountering him to ask his medical opinion of their ailments.

''Yep, that's okay, too,'' he answered as if it honestly didn't bother him. ''As okay as it is that with everybody in town knowing my home phone number there also aren't many who will hesitate to use it if they're sick in the middle of the night or on my day off. I guess I get to be everyone's mother,'' he finished with a laugh.

But Emmy hadn't seen anything about him that reminded her of a mother. As far as she could tell, he was all man.

And the more brandy she drank, the more aware of that she was.

Which didn't seem all that wise.

So she set the brandy glass on the coffee table

and said, "The upstairs will be warm by now. I should go."

Aiden didn't say anything to stop her, and Emmy felt a twinge of utterly uncalled-for disappointment.

Instead he set his glass on the coffee table, too, and got up as she did to walk her to the door.

"I open the office at eight in the morning," he said along the way. "If that's too early for you, I can get my nurse to come out and pick up Mickey and me, and you can use my car to come in later. Noon, if that's what works for you."

He was smiling a wicked smile and she knew he was giving her a hard time about sleeping until nearly noon that morning. But the smile was too enticing to make her take offense, and Emmy just laughed.

"I was hoping you thought I was up there busy with paperwork or something."

"Nope."

"Well, pretend you did," she said, wondering at the flirtatious tone in her own voice. Then she amended it to add, "Eight o'clock tomorrow is fine."

"Better be down here about a quarter till," he said with a full grin that announced he was enjoying this.

But then so was she. The banter. The teasing. The sight of that slightly long hair combed away from his strikingly handsome face. Those light-blue eyes that were sparkling with mischief and staring down at her so intently.

So intently everything seemed to stand still, and she suddenly wondered what he was thinking.

If he might be thinking about kissing her.

Or was the thought of Aiden kissing her just going through her mind? Along with maybe a tiny wish that he would....

But he didn't make any move in that direction. He stayed standing straight and tall, not so much as leaning toward her, to give even a hint that that might be what he was considering.

It was only on her mind, she decided.

And it shouldn't have been. It definitely shouldn't have been.

So she reached for the door handle, not realizing that Aiden's hand was already there.

Sparks of static electricity shot from her to him but it felt like something more than that that skittered along her nerve endings, and she yanked her hand back in a hurry.

"Sorry," she muttered.

But he didn't even flinch. He just went on staring at her as he opened the door for her and then reached out to push open the screen, too.

Emmy slipped out onto the porch as if she were escaping something.

"Thanks for dinner," she said, trying to defuse what felt remarkably like sexual tension in the air between them.

"Thanks for helping with Mickey while I set up the crib," he countered.

"Sure. I'll see you in the morning."

"I'll see *you* in the morning."

Emmy raised her hand in a little wave and then

wasted no time getting around to the side stairs to go up to her own room.

And as she did, she felt as if she really *had* escaped something.

She'd escaped her own very unprofessional thoughts.

And the even more unprofessional desires that had gone with them.

Chapter Three

When the phone rang at seven the next morning, Aiden made a dive for it and picked it up before it could ring again. Mickey was still asleep, and that was how Aiden wanted him, at least until he finished shaving.

"I thought I might wake you up, not catch you in the middle of a fifty-yard dash," the voice on the other end said in answer to Aiden's breathless hello.

"Ethan," Aiden said, recognizing his older brother's voice.

He switched the phone to his other ear and took it with him to the bathroom to lather his face and shave while they talked.

"How was the honeymoon?" he asked along the way.

"Perfect," Ethan answered enthusiastically. "We did a little sight-seeing, a little swimming, a little fishing, some lying around on the beach, a lot of other things...."

"Well, it was your honeymoon, after all," Aiden said to his brother's innuendo, and they both laughed.

Ethan had only recently reconnected with Paris Hanley, a woman he'd had a brief fling with and who—he discovered fourteen months later—had produced a beautiful baby girl named Hannah. One thing had led to another and Ethan and Paris had gotten married two weeks ago.

"I hate that I missed the wedding," Aiden said, meaning it.

"Did your patient die?"

"She did. The day after. I just couldn't leave her. She was 103 years old and she'd outlived all her friends and relatives. If I hadn't been with her, she would have died alone."

"Hey, I understand. That's one of the reasons I'm calling—to tell you I'm sending the videotape of the whole thing. You'll have it in a day or two, and then you'll feel like you were there."

"Great. Devon said it was a nice wedding. Good food, terrific cake, a big bash of a party."

"It was."

"Have you decided where you're going to live yet?" Aiden asked then.

"Pretty much. I think we're going to settle in Dunbar."

Dunbar was the small town east of Denver where

Aiden and his two brothers had grown up. It was also where Ethan had a large estate.

"Paris's mom has finally agreed to move there," Ethan continued. "Leaving her alone in Denver was what was keeping Paris from agreeing before. We still can't convince her to live *with* us no matter how hard we try. She's sure she'd be intruding. So I'm going to have a place built on the grounds for her."

Aiden knew Paris was close to her mother. They'd been sharing a place to make ends meet before Ethan's reentry into Paris's life. But making ends meet wouldn't be a problem for them anymore. Ethan had started his own computer software company when computers were just beginning to take over the world. The company was multinational now, and Ethan would never have to worry about money.

"Devon was up here last week," Aiden said then. "He needed some pictures of bears for an article in *National Geographic*."

Their younger brother was a wildlife photographer.

"He told me he was headed up there. Where is he now?"

"He went across into Canada on Friday. Said he might come back through here again before he heads for home."

"I thought he was going to stay with you the whole time."

"He was. But then I got word that the director of the Bernsdorf Foundation was coming up this week and he figured he'd be in the way. As it turns out, things are so complicated he was better off leaving."

"How are things complicated?"

"You won't believe it when I tell you."

Aiden laid out the whole story of Mickey's appearance, including the possibility that the baby could be his.

"You're kidding. What are the odds of two of us having a kid we don't know about?"

"Before this I'd have said the odds were astronomical. Now, maybe not so astronomical."

"Are you taking care of the baby on your own?" Ethan asked.

"Not much choice," Aiden said.

"Do you know what you're doing?"

"I did double rotations in pediatrics. I can change a diaper and heat a bottle, yeah."

"And do you really think this baby is yours?"

"I honestly don't know," Aiden repeated. "I'm just trying to figure it out one way or another. Speaking of which, didn't you say that the minute you set eyes on Hannah you thought she was yours?"

"I was pretty sure, yes. But then you saw her yourself when you were down here—she looks so much like Mom."

"Yeah, well, Mickey doesn't look like anyone I know."

"But there's the timetable and the fact that he was left with you," Ethan reminded.

"I know, those are both things I have to take into consideration. But what about the way you *felt*, Ethan? It seemed like you felt some kind of bond. Some emotional tie that clinched it for you."

"There was something there," Ethan admitted. "Are you feeling that?"

"No. I mean, don't get me wrong, he's a nice baby. But I didn't feel any instant attachment or bond, or anything *parental*."

"If he's yours I'm sure that will come," Ethan reasoned.

"*If* he's mine."

"But you're not really hoping he is."

"If he is, he is, but no, I can't say I'm *hoping* he is. Although Emmy and I did have a good time with him yesterday, showing him off as if he were ours while—"

"Whoa! Emmy? Who's Emmy? A new woman in your life?"

"No," Aiden said as if his brother had lost his mind. "Emmy Harris. She's the Bernsdorf Foundation's director. I told you she was coming up here this week."

"The way you just referred to her wasn't the way I would have referred to someone in her position. Is something *else* going on up there?"

"I'm just showing her around, letting her see where Boonesbury would use the grant money. What *else* would be going on?"

"'Emmy and I had a good time with him yesterday, showing him off as if he were our own,'" Ethan said, repeating Aiden's words back to him. "That sounded couple-ish and a hell of a lot friendlier than I'd be with somebody who's essentially a business associate."

"Maybe you just took it wrong."

"Maybe not. What are the particulars on this woman?"

"The particulars?" Aiden asked.

"Age, weight, height, hair color, pretty, not pretty, wart on her nose—the particulars."

"She's late twenties, slim, about five-four, reddish-brown hair, hazel eyes, no warts, definitely pretty."

"Pretty enough to have you looking twice?" Ethan inquired with some insinuation in his tone.

"Sure," Aiden confirmed as if it were no big deal.

"And you like her?" Ethan probed further.

"Well enough."

"Well enough to be showing off a baby with her."

"I'm not dumb enough to try seducing the woman who could make or break our getting the grant, if that's what you're fishing around about," Aiden said, cutting to the chase.

"Was that what I was fishing around about? Or is that just what you've been thinking about?"

Aiden laughed, wiping the last of the cream from his face, since he actually had managed to shave while they'd been talking. "Okay, maybe I've done a little thinking about seducing her. But I'm not going to do it."

"You should."

"Bad advice."

"This is the first time I've heard you interested in someone since Rebecca—excluding the drunken night with this Nora woman because one night doesn't constitute interest so much as bodily need."

"If there even *was* something between Nora and me," Aiden felt inclined to qualify.

Ethan ignored it to continue making his point about Emmy. "But your attraction to this foundation director is something I think you should pursue."

"At the possible expense of a six-hundred-thousand-dollar grant? I don't think so," Aiden said.

"If romancing her costs you the grant I'll donate the money myself," his brother offered as incentive.

"You've done enough for Boonesbury. You should own the whole town for what you've put in here already. It's about time they find another benefactor."

"I'm serious, A."

"So am I. Besides, Emmy Harris is about the last woman I should waste time pursuing. She seems like even more of a city girl than Rebecca was. She didn't even bring a coat, and she thought the conditions she found here were a joke Howard Wilson was playing on her. Unless I've missed my call, more than two blocks from a Bloomingdales is wilderness to her. And she doesn't like it one bit. No way is she a candidate for seducing, whether I'm attracted to her or not. It would be as much of a disaster as Rebecca was."

"So you *are* attracted to her," Ethan said, selectively not hearing the rest.

"It doesn't matter."

"Oh, it matters," Ethan said smugly.

"I'm telling you, it doesn't."

"Attractions have a way of making themselves matter."

"Not when you don't let them. And I'm not letting this one. I have my hands full right now, it would cost Boonesbury too much, and in the end I'd just get my heart stomped on again. No, thanks."

"My offer still stands," Ethan said as if he hadn't put any stock whatsoever in any of Aiden's denials.

"I'll keep that in mind," Aiden said facetiously.

Mickey had been stirring for the last few minutes and the baby finally let out a louder cry to let it be known he was awake.

"Is that the baby I hear?" Ethan asked.

"It isn't my stomach growling."

"I better let you go then. I'll check in with you in a few days. But in the meantime let nature take its course with the foundation lady."

"No," Aiden said firmly.

He meant it, too. Even after he and Ethan had exchanged goodbyes and ended the call.

His attraction to Emmy Harris had three strikes against it—the grant, the mess with Mickey and what he had no doubt was a total difference in lifestyle.

And three strikes ruled it out. Completely.

No, it didn't change the fact that he was enjoying every minute of her company. It didn't change the fact that he couldn't seem to get her off his mind. Or that he was as eager as a kid on the way to the circus to see her again.

But he was doing his best to ignore it all.

He just wished his best worked a little better....

By the time Aiden's office closed at six-thirty that evening, Emmy had seen the first indications that

Boonesbury was in need of serious improvements when it came to their medical care.

She'd spent the day following Aiden around, talking to his patients and his nurse, Maria, and on the legal pad she was using to take notes she had a long list of what the grant money would be used for.

Already she knew there was a need for a generator so that power outages didn't destroy whole supplies of refrigerated medications and vaccines. There was a need for better office facilities that would increase the examining rooms from the two tiny ones that were now all there was. There was the need for a well-equipped surgical suite for out-patient procedures and a room for overnight stays when necessary. There was a need for a centrifuge. A new EKG machine. A more sophisticated X-ray machine and an even rudimentary ultrasound imaging machine. There was a need for both an incubator for newborns and an incubator to cultivate cultures to test for bacteria. There was a need for a general replacement of equipment that was outdated by about twenty years.

But in spite of the environment and the old tools of the trade, Emmy couldn't help being impressed by Aiden's skills as a physician.

He was calm and kind and patient. He listened and never hurried anyone, even when his waiting room was jam-packed. And he was an adept, insightful, skillful, inspired medical practitioner whose knowledge far exceeded the primitive conditions he worked under.

And that didn't have anything to do with the fact that he looked drop-dead gorgeous in the gray twill slacks, dove-gray dress shirt and charcoal necktie that gave him a more professional appearance than Emmy had seen from him until then.

In fact, appreciating how good he looked was something she had to fight all day long so she could do her job.

It helped to have so many other people around, though. Aiden hadn't been kidding when he'd said Mondays were busy. People streamed in the whole time, most of them with ailments but without appointments.

Plus there was Maria, Aiden's nurse, office manager and receptionist, and, of course Mickey, who was a big distraction and the star attraction.

As he had been on Sunday at the inn, the infant was perfectly comfortable with strangers. It was a good thing since it seemed as if nearly everyone who came into the office wanted to hold him, play with him or feed him. There were even a few who were willing to change him when the need arose.

No one knew who he was or had any information about Nora Finley, but there was no shortage of willingness to pitch in or to offer to help care for him if Aiden couldn't. It surprised Emmy to see so many people willing to take an active role and get involved.

When Aiden had finally finished with the last patient, he had Maria hold Mickey while he took a drop of his blood to determine the little boy's type.

Maria made sure Mickey was calmed down and

happy again before she said good-night and left Emmy alone with doctor and baby once more.

"Well, what's the verdict?" Emmy asked when Aiden rejoined her and Mickey in the waiting room where Mickey was secure in his car seat as Emmy dangled plastic keys in front of him to occupy him.

"He has my blood type," Aiden answered.

"Oh." Emmy's tone wasn't any happier than she felt to hear that, although she knew she had no reason to care one way or another.

Then Aiden added, "It isn't conclusive, though. It's the most common blood type there is. And since I did have Nora's blood type in her file and it's the same as Mickey's, the only way it would have been conclusive proof that he isn't mine would have been a different blood type."

"But as it is, he still could or couldn't be yours."

"Right."

Emmy leaned close to Mickey and said, "I think maybe he stuck you for nothing."

"I did not," Aiden defended himself from Emmy's joke. Then he took one of Mickey's feet to wiggle and said, "She's just giving me a hard time, don't pay any attention to her."

Mickey didn't have to be told not to pay any attention to Emmy. He was too delighted to have Aiden in sight. He was grinning up at the big man with adoring eyes.

"I think all is forgiven," Emmy said. "Of course, it doesn't hurt that he seems to have developed baby hero worship—if there is such a thing."

''Oh, he's just workin' me,'' Aiden said.

But Emmy could tell that he liked how the infant seemed to adore him. That he might even like Mickey more than he was ready to admit.

Then he said, ''How about we get out of here? I have a couple of steaks in the refrigerator that we can put on the broiler, and we can have a nice, quiet night back at the cabin.''

It had been a long day and nothing sounded better to Emmy, so she agreed without a second thought.

Once they had Mickey dressed in his snowsuit and again bundled amidst blankets in the baby carrier, Aiden turned off all the lights and locked up, and they headed for home.

During the drive they turned on the radio to see if Aiden's message was going out. The cabin was within view before they heard it, but there was a full report on Mickey—complete with his description, the fact that he'd been left with Aiden and that any information regarding him would be greatly appreciated.

Then the disc jockey went on to relay Aiden's request for Nora Finley to contact him, and that took on some innuendo.

''Now, no more calls, people. Every time I've aired this today somebody's phoned in to ask do I know if these two things are connected. All's I *do* know is that the doc is real anxious to hear from you, Nora, and we're all wonderin' if it could be that little Mickey is yours. Yours and the doc's maybe? Hmmm…''

Emmy looked at Aiden as he came to a stop in

front of the cabin, curious as to what his response to the public teasing was.

He turned off the radio, cut the engine, and then glanced her way from the corner of his eye as if he knew what was on her mind. "Anything and everything is pretty much fair game up here," he said. "You have to learn not to take things too seriously."

Which apparently he had learned because another man might not have had such an easy time letting it roll off his back.

But somehow the fact that Aiden did was just one more thing Emmy liked about him.

Then he let himself out of the SUV and unfastened Mickey's seat while Emmy got out, too, and that seemed to be the end of the subject.

Once they were all inside the cabin again, Aiden removed Mickey's outerwear.

"You know," he said, "if one of us cooks and the other feeds Mickey, we'll get to eat a lot quicker."

"Okay, but just in case this really is a test Howard has arranged, I want it duly noted that I have already put in a long day of work for the foundation and I did not give in to distractions before I was finished with it."

"Duly noted," Aiden said with an amused expression. "What do you want? KP or baby duty?"

Not great options for Emmy.

"The extent of my culinary expertise is microwaving food that comes out of a box," she warned. "So you probably don't want me cooking."

"Baby duty, then," he concluded, surprising her by handing Mickey over without ceremony.

Reflex made her accept him, but it was the first time she'd actually held the baby. And although she'd been watching Aiden and a whole lot of other people do it for the past two days, she still didn't take to it like a duck to water.

She didn't really know what to do with him.

"Uh, are you sure it's baby duty you want?" Aiden asked when he saw that she merely went on holding the little boy the way she'd received him—her hands under his arms, her elbows extended.

"I can't cook," she repeated, letting him know this had only become her choice as the lesser of two evils.

"Doesn't look like you have much experience with baby care, either."

"None."

"You never baby-sat as a teenager?"

"I worked in my father's office as a teenager."

"Okay, well, since Mickey isn't a wet cat, let's start by shifting him a little. Pull him into your body, onto your hip. Let some of his weight rest there and on your forearm, and hold his back with your other hand."

Emmy felt really stupid to have to be taught something so rudimentary, but she followed his instructions and finally had Mickey more comfortably and securely positioned.

But both the need for Aiden to instruct her and the lack of aplomb with which she'd accomplished the task must not have convinced him she was suited for solo baby duty because he said, "I'll tell you what, I'll walk you through the basics of Mickey and then I'll cook. I'm not starving yet, anyway, and a later dinner might be better. After Mickey's down for the count. Then, if you're ever stranded on an island with a baby you'll know what to do."

Emmy saw through his diplomacy, but she appreciated it just the same and decided to pretend she didn't see through it and just go along with it.

Learning what to do with Mickey turned out to be fun, though. It was more like they were playing with him than anything, and Emmy ended up doing the actual feeding, bathing and getting him ready for bed, with Aiden only acting as her coach.

And although Mickey had an obvious preference for Aiden, through the process he warmed up to Emmy, too, and left her amazed by how much his little smiles and giggles could warm her heart and by how good it felt to have him snuggle against her as she fed him his bottle and he began to fall asleep in her arms.

When he did, Emmy and Aiden put Mickey in his crib, tucking him in and sharing a silent moment watching him sleep before they turned off the light and quietly padded out of the room.

"Okay, *now* I'm starved. How about you?" Aiden said as they went to the kitchen.

"I decided I must be hungry when the strained peas looked good to me," Emmy confessed.

The two of them shared the cooking chore, too, with Aiden teaching her a few basics about preparing steaks just the way he'd taught her about caring for Mickey.

It was almost eight-thirty before they sat down to eat the beautifully broiled meat, salad and rolls the joint effort produced. As Aiden poured them each a glass of wine to go with it all, he said, "So how did you come to this advanced age without baby-wrangling experience or cooking skills?"

Emmy shrugged. "I told you I worked for my father instead of baby-sitting when I was a teenager. And since I don't have any kids of my own and I was an only child, where would I have gained baby-wrangling experience?"

"Okay, fair enough. But what about cooking? Haven't you needed to eat?"

"Sure. But my mother died when I was three, and my dad never learned so he couldn't teach me. As an adult I practice what he *did* teach me—nuking frozen dinners, how to order takeout or make reservations at the best restaurants."

"That's bad," Aiden said with that deep, rich laugh of his that made something skitter along the surface of her skin.

"We just weren't a baby or a cooking family," Emmy defended with a laugh of her own, appreciating that he wasn't really finding fault with her lack of domesticity the way her former husband had.

"So there was only you and your father from when you were three years old?"

"He dated here and there. But mostly it was just Dad and me, yes."

"What did he do for a living?"

"He was a doctor. A cardio-thoracic surgeon."

That raised Aiden's eyebrows. "Would I know him?"

"Maybe. He was well published in the *Journal of American Medicine*. Edward Harris."

"I do know him. Well, I know *of* him. I read some of his articles when I was in school and I had an attending physician on one of my rotations who had been a resident under him. She said if she ever needed heart surgery she'd travel to the ends of the earth for him to be the one to do it. Is he still in practice?"

"No. He passed away about six years ago. It was one of those ugly ironies—he died of a heart attack. But at least it was in his sleep and he didn't suffer."

"Is there a connection between what he did and you ending up giving out grants for the medically underprivileged?"

Emmy liked that Aiden was astute enough to put that together.

"There is a connection, as a matter of fact. My dad actually started the Bernsdorf Foundation on behalf of Alastair Bernsdorf. He was a patient and a friend. They were fishing buddies like you and Howard. Alastair—Al—and my dad were fishing near a small town in Colorado when Al had a heart attack. My dad barely managed to keep him alive until a helicopter could airlift them to the city because the small town didn't have a medical facility. When Al died ten years later he left his fortune to Dad to use to rectify that situation where he could. So Dad started the foundation.''

''And you had to work your way up the ladder, anyway?''

''I did. I was only about sixteen when the foundation was formed. I was working in my dad's office—filing, cleaning up, making sure the examining rooms were stocked—and when they opened the foundation's offices Dad loaned me to them to help set things up. I wasn't supposed to stay, but when I was there I wasn't the doctor's daughter, I was accepted as myself. I liked that and so I switched from doing detail work at Dad's office to doing it at the foundation office. After a while I decided I wanted a business degree so I could work there doing more than the detail work. Unfortunately, I also decided I *didn't* want to be a doctor the way my father wanted me to.''

''Bet that disappointed him.''

''Thoroughly. In fact, I think he made Howard keep me doing grunt work as long as possible in the hope that I'd eventually get discouraged and go to medical school after all.''

''But you were stubborn.'' Something about that seemed to amuse Aiden again because he gave her one of the devilish smiles that made his blue eyes sparkle all the more.

''Stubborn has such a negative sound to it,'' Emmy said with a mischievous smile of her own. ''Let's just say I was tenacious enough to stick it out and work hard and badger my way into more and more responsibilities until I finally convinced my father and Howard that I was not going to be a doctor.''

''And then you were made director?''

''Oh, no. I was still a long way from that. I definitely worked my way up. At one time or another I've done just about every job there is to do there. And then I took a sort of hiatus for a couple of years when I didn't work for the foundation at all.'' But she didn't want to go into that so she didn't explain. ''When that was over and I came back to the foundation Evelyn Wright had just been hired as director and I was made assistant director.''

''But Evelyn Wright was wrong for the job?'' he suggested with a laugh at his own bad pun.

It suddenly occurred to Emmy that maybe she was talking too much.

''Am I boring you to death with all this?''

''Not at all.''

She searched his handsome face to see if he was telling the truth. But she didn't find any indication that he wished she'd shut up. Instead his focus was all on her, and he was so attentive he really did seem interested in what she was saying. In getting to know her.

It was nice and Emmy couldn't help appreciating that about him even though she knew her will to resist her attraction to him was probably weakening.

''I remember you said some things Saturday night about why this Evelyn didn't make it as director,'' he said, reminding Emmy that that was what they were talking about.

It was also nice to know he'd been listening close enough even from the start to recall what she'd said.

"Evelyn was good with paperwork," Emmy explained. "But when it came to the fieldwork she wasn't."

"You said she freaked out over the trips themselves, that she took everything too seriously and—"

He really had been listening. But Emmy didn't need it all recited back to her so she stopped him before he had the chance to.

"Right. Evelyn didn't like the inconveniences and discomforts she found on these trips, and she was easily swept up into the hardships or other problems she came across. She'd end up trying to fix everything and everybody. And then there was the near crash of the small plane she was on, and that was it for her. She quit the minute she got back."

"And you got your chance."

"Mmm. Two months ago. But not without a fight even then. Howard still thought I was too young for the job. Evelyn was in her late forties and that seemed about right to him."

"So you put your hair in a bun and proved him wrong."

"*Hopefully* I'll prove him wrong—this is my first time out, remember? Or did I not tell you that before?"

It didn't seem to matter whether or not she'd told him before, because he didn't address that. He just said, "Well, I'd put my money on you. Even without the bun."

They'd finished eating by then and since it was getting late Emmy suggested they do the dishes.

Aiden washed and Emmy dried, and while they did Aiden backtracked slightly to the subject they'd floated over earlier.

"So, speaking of flying in a small plane…"

"I'm okay not speaking of it, thanks, anyway."

Aiden laughed. "I'm afraid I have to. Tuesdays are my days to visit my outlying patients. And that's how I do it—flying is the quickest way."

"You want me to stay here and watch Mickey?" Emmy said with false hope.

"Maria's offered to keep Mickey for me. I thought you'd want to see that aspect of what goes on around here."

Emmy was supposed to see every aspect of what went on around here. Medically, at least. But that didn't make her any more thrilled about flying in that small plane.

"In other words," she said, "I need to go and I don't have a choice but to fly. In your little plane."

The dishes were done and Aiden reached for the towel she still held to dry his hands.

But for some unknown reason Emmy didn't let go of it. She hung on to her end and there they stood, joined by that dish towel hanging between them like a Maypole ribbon.

"I really am a good pilot," Aiden reminded in a confidential tone that somehow seemed very sexy even though the message wasn't.

"Right. Like you'd admit it if you weren't," she

joked, surprised to hear the same tone in her own voice.

"I got you here in one piece, didn't I?"

"Just lucky," she responded, trying to ignore the little wave of arousal that was beginning to wash through her.

"Pure skill," he countered with a half smile as his eyes held hers. "I promise a safe trip. Both ways."

For a moment Emmy didn't realize "both ways" meant the flight out and back again. She thought it meant something entirely different. As if one way he was promising her a safe trip was in the air. And maybe the other was in bed....

Then she rectified that outrageous thought in a hurry, wondering what was going on with her.

"I'll hold you to that," she warned. Meaning she was going to hold him to the safe trip in the plane.

But when he said, "Okay," there was an insinuative edge to it that once more made it seem as if he might have known what she was thinking.

But whether he did or not, the bottom line was that somehow along the way this had begun to feel like a date. A very good date.

A date that might have reached the moment when they would share a kiss that would come as easily as all their teasing had. As all their banter had. As all their flirting had.

As easily as he seemed to find it to probe her eyes with his gorgeous blue ones.

As easily as she found it to stare up into that face that was so handsome it made her pulse race.

As easily as he found it to move a little closer to her, to lean just a tad nearer as she tilted her chin ever so slightly in his direction....

But then it was as if he came to his senses.

Because suddenly he straightened up, broke their eye contact, dropped the towel that had connected them, and said in a much more neutral tone, "Honestly, I'm a good pilot and I won't let anything happen."

Emmy drew back slightly herself, embarrassed and chagrined that she had even been thinking what she had.

"Okay," she conceded too quickly, too awkwardly.

Then, in an attempt to regain her equilibrium, she said, "What time do you want to leave?"

"I usually try to get out of here early, but with Mickey I don't think I can make it before eight," he answered, his voice slightly raspy now. And maybe a little stressed.

"Eight it is, then," she agreed, hurrying to the living room portion of the cabin as if setting their departure time had forced her into fast action.

But if Aiden found it odd, he didn't say anything. Instead, as she put on her coat, he said, "Don't wear anything too nice. We'll be hiking some."

"Jeans and comfortable shoes it is," she confirmed.

Then she went to the door. Still in a hurry.

"See you at eight."

"Right."

Aiden hadn't budged from his spot in the kitchen to walk her out or open the door for her or any of what he'd done the night before. Any of what he might have done if this *had* been a date.

But Emmy thought she knew why.

She didn't think he was being rude, she just thought that he was trying to make sure neither of them was tempted a second time to do what they both knew they shouldn't do.

And it was just as well.

So she said a clipped good-night to him from the distance and he answered the same way before she let herself out and went upstairs to the attic room that neither of them had thought to preheat.

But that was okay, too.

Because the chill of the small space when she got there did wonders to bring Emmy to her senses. It helped her remember all the things she knew better than to lose sight of.

Like the fact that she was in Boonesbury on business. Boonesbury, where she would never choose to vacation let alone live, the way Aiden did.

Like the fact that she had already been involved with one man who wanted a different lifestyle than she did and it had proved disastrous.

Like the fact that at that exact moment Aiden Tarlington could have a child of his own making, sleeping downstairs in his bedroom. A child he hadn't expected to have and might now have to raise all on his own.

It was just that, even remembering all that didn't chase away the image of him in her mind.

Of him standing so close in front of her at his kitchen sink, tall and muscular and masculine. Incredible to look at. Incredible to be with.

And so simmeringly sexy that she could still feel the heat of him as if he'd left an imprint on her.

Chapter Four

The breathtaking beauty of Alaska was almost enough to keep Emmy's mind off her nervousness about flying in Aiden's small plane the next day, after they'd dropped Mickey off with Maria.

Snowcapped mountains framed verdant fields of evergreens and cobalt-blue lakes surrounded by umber foliage in its last blush of Alaska's autumn.

If Emmy had been more of an outdoorswoman she might have felt as though she'd happened upon a rich cache of hiking, biking, climbing and canoeing opportunities. As it was, she just tried not to think about something going wrong with the plane, about crashing into the vast unpopulated wilderness, and instead attempted to merely enjoy the scenery.

The scenery outside, at least.

Inside the cockpit she was putting effort into *not* noticing the scenery—namely a freshly laundered Aiden.

He was dressed in mountain boots, heavy jeans, a turtleneck under a crew-neck sweater, and a leather aviator's jacket.

His hair was casually combed into place. His angular, sharply planed face was cleanly shaven. And he smelled like the woods in spring—wonderful enough to make even a city girl entertain fantasies of camp outs.

"The plane is where a good chunk of the grant money would be spent," he said after they'd been in the air for a while, drawing her out of her appreciation of the way he looked and smelled.

But not without some difficulty.

"Right now the repairs and upkeep are mostly coming out of my pocket," Aiden was saying. "And the plane isn't equipped the way it should be. It should be outfitted for emergencies and airlifts of critical patients—like a hospital helicopter. But as it is, I have my medical bag, a few supplies, and that's about it."

By then Emmy had her mind back in line. "What did you mean when you said you and Boonesbury are partners in owning the plane?" she asked.

"Just that. The county raised what it could for the plane because we needed it, but they came in short by about a third. I had some savings so I put up the rest of the money and it's licensed under my name.

Plus, like I said, I foot the maintenance-and-repair bills.''

"What if you were to leave? Who would have first claim to the plane?"

"I'm not leaving," he said without hesitation. "I've made my home here. I've bought land where I'm going to start building my own house next spring. I'm here to stay."

"*Nothing* could make you leave?" Emmy said, prompted by more than just the foundation's business. By something personal lurking beneath her professional duty to ask.

"Nothing I can think of."

"Let's say something monumental does persuade you to leave Boonesbury—for instance, you marry Nora Finley and she becomes president of the United States and you have to go to Washington...."

Aiden took his eyes off the skyline to look at her. "I am not going to marry Nora Finley," he said definitively. And maybe a little defensively, too.

"This is hypothetical," Emmy pointed out.

"I wouldn't even marry Nora Finley hypothetically."

He sounded adamant, and it soothed something in Emmy that shouldn't have been ruffled. But still, for the sake of the grant, she needed to know about the future of the plane.

So, with elaborately patient enunciation, she said, "Okay, if something—anything—dragged you away from Boonesbury, what would happen to this aircraft?"

"Oh, I get it. You're wanting to make sure that if grant money goes into it, it stays in Boonesbury," he said. "Well, don't worry, it would. I have an agreement with the county that even if I left, I couldn't take the plane with me. So that isn't an issue." He paused a moment but for some reason felt inclined to say again, "But I'm not going anywhere."

"Got it," she assured.

Loud and clear. Like a warning alarm. Aiden Tarlington was not leaving Boonesbury.

And that was something Emmy knew she shouldn't forget.

They again landed in an open field rather than at any kind of airport. Only this time there was someone there to meet them—a burly man dressed in jeans and a jean jacket.

The tawny color of his skin, his waist-length black hair—braided into two thin braids that fell in front of his shoulders—and the beaded band around his brawny neck told Emmy he was a Native American.

He was standing on the running board of an old blue truck, waving enthusiastically, as if they might overlook him otherwise. And as soon as the engines were cut, he rushed to Emmy's side of the plane to help her out.

"Emmy Harris, this is White Eagle Lawson. We all call him Law. Law, this is Emmy Harris from the Bernsdorf Foundation," Aiden said as he made note of his gauge readings and then got out of the plane, too.

"Happy to meetcha," White Eagle Lawson said in a surprisingly high-pitched voice.

"Law lugs me around from house call to house call when I'm up here," Aiden explained. Then he motioned toward the old truck. "And our coach awaits."

Emmy rode between the two men in the cab of the truck as they traveled across bumpy paved roads and some that were barely more than rutted dirt paths. But despite being in the presence of them both, she was only really aware of Aiden. Of how near his thigh was to hers. Of the scent of that aftershave. Of the heat his big body gave off and of how much she liked being warmed by it.

There were no distractions in the company. The two men discussed where they were going today and who Aiden needed to see, so Emmy was effectively excluded from the conversation. And left to her own devices, her mind wandered even more persistently to Aiden. To fantasies of putting his close proximity to good use. Of having him reach a long arm around her to bring her even nearer. Of laying her head on his substantial shoulder. Of having him pull her snugly into his side where she might nuzzle that thick neck of his. Or nibble his ear…

Scenery, she thought, desperately trying to find something else to focus on so she could escape the torment of her own mind.

But counting fir trees was hardly enough and she was grateful when they finally reached their first stop. Even if it was nothing more than a scant clearing in the forest they'd been driving through. A scant clearing where a tiny, dilapidated cottage nestled alone among the pine trees.

Once the engine was off Law pulled a newspaper from behind the visor above the windshield and seemed to settle in to wait like a chauffeur who had delivered his charges.

It left Emmy wondering if she was supposed to do the same.

Until Aiden climbed out of the truck and said, "Law doesn't like to come in with me."

"But it's okay if I do?" Emmy asked.

"Sure," he said as if he hadn't considered anything else.

She wasn't as convinced that that was the best idea. She might have been better off sitting outside with Law, gathering her resistance during Aiden's absences.

But that wasn't her job, she reminded herself. Her job was to see for herself what the medical needs of this community were, and she couldn't do that by staying in the truck.

So she got out, too, and took a few deep breaths in hopes of clearing her mind.

"Feels good to breathe in this cold, clean air, doesn't it?" Aiden said as if he were pitching the positive aspects of the area.

"Mmm," Emmy agreed, glad he thought she was merely enjoying the lack of pollution.

But unfortunately the air didn't act as much of an antidote to his appeal, because as he led the way to the old frame house, Emmy's eyes went to his derriere, and a whole new appreciation rippled through her.

"'Bout time you got here," a booming, craggy voice called as they climbed the steps to the porch.

Emmy tore her gaze from Aiden's rear end in a hurry and found the source of the remark—a surprisingly frail-looking woman who stood in the lee of the front door and held open the screen for them.

The woman was very short—at least an inch under five feet tall. Her back was bent, her white hair was sparse and stuck out every which way, and her face had more wrinkles and grooves than a prune. But she had applied a bright pink lipstick to her lips.

"Hello, Agnes, my only love," Aiden greeted her affectionately.

"I better be your only love," the ancient woman countered as they all went inside the musty-smelling house where a large husky watched them enter from where he was curled on a braided rug near the fireplace.

As he had with Law, Aiden introduced Emmy to Agnes LaToya. And to her dog, Dog.

"Emmy is checking things out to see if we qualify for some grant money to modernize the medical care I can offer," he informed the woman.

Agnes LaToya looked Emmy up and down, made a sucking sound from the corner of her mouth and then said, "You can sit over on the hearth, out of the way."

Emmy got the message—she'd been dispatched like the house pet to the same area.

And once she had joined Dog the dog, the older woman seemed to forget her presence altogether as she led Aiden to the sofa where she put her energy into gruffly flirting with him.

Since Aiden was there to check the arthritis in Agnes's knuckles, he did his examination right there in the living room, with Emmy observing from the distance of the fireplace.

"When are you going to move into Boonesbury?" he said as he did.

"Not goin' to," the elderly woman answered as if this were a conversation they'd had many times before.

"If you were in town and something happened to you, I could get to you faster. But out here..." Aiden let his voice dwindle off ominously.

"I got Dog. I could send 'im down the road for help."

"Dog might meet Girl Dog and leave you here to rot."

"Not Dog. He's a good ol' boy."

Aiden shook his head. "You're a hard woman, Aggy."

"Not all over," she said, with a voice full of insinuation that made Aiden laugh.

He gave up on that subject as he seemed to conclude his exam and said, "I brought you a new topical cream to try. You rub it in like lotion."

He took a tube out of his medical bag, but rather than accepting it, Agnes LaToya extended both arms. "You do it."

There was a sly bent to that command, but Aiden just laughed and shook his head again as he opened the medicine and squeezed a dab of the ointment into his palm. Then he began to apply it to her fingers, and Agnes tossed a glance at Emmy.

"The guy's got great hands," she said out of the corner of her mouth.

Emmy tried to maintain her professionalism but part of her wanted to laugh at the old woman and the other part of her wanted to try the same gambit. After all, from the looks of it, Agnes was right—Aiden did have great hands. Strong, agile hands that seemed to massage the other woman with just the right combination of gentleness and pressure.

Strength and agility and gentleness and pressure that Emmy suddenly craved to feel herself.

On much more intimate portions of her body than her hands...

Or maybe she'd just completely lost her mind. What other reason could there be for feeling jealous of a woman old enough to be her great-grandmother? For pining for the touch of a man she barely knew? Maybe the Alaskan air was *too* clean. Maybe she needed a little pollution in her lungs to keep her sane.

But sane or insane, it did look appealing to have those hands of his working a little magic....

From Agnes LaToya's place Law drove for another half hour before reaching their next stop, and that became the pattern of the day—a not-short drive through unspoiled wilderness to reach a single house or trailer or cabin where there were no other signs of civilization.

The patients Aiden saw were an eclectic bunch— young and old, male and female, a few obviously well educated and others who could barely read or write, some loners, others with families, and one group of eleven people who lived a communal lifestyle.

About the only thing they all had in common was their warm welcome of Aiden.

But Emmy could see why. Besides the fact that he really was a good doctor, his bedside manner varied with the personalities of his patients to make them comfortable. Sometimes he was nurturing, other times he was teasing and humorous, and when the patient called for it, he merely spoke man-to-man.

It was interesting to watch. And Emmy couldn't help being even more impressed by him than she'd been the previous day in his office.

Dusk had fallen before they'd visited all the people they needed to, but once that last patient had been seen, Aiden instructed Law to take them to Nora Finley's cabin.

Emmy shot Aiden a questioning glance, and in answer to it, he said, "Her place is not too much farther up the road. We might as well check it out while we're here."

Nora Finley's *place* was a log cabin no bigger than the size of a single car garage. Full darkness was upon them when they reached it, and there was no light visible through the only window.

Yet still Law pulled to a stop a few feet from the

front door and Aiden said to Emmy, "Let's take a look inside."

"Since it doesn't look as if Nora Finley is here, I think that's considered breaking and entering even in the middle of nowhere," she said.

It was Law who answered that one. "Nora leaves the door unlocked in case somebody passin' by needs shelter. Most folks around here do the same. She don't care if you go on in."

Which was what Aiden was intent on doing because he got out of the truck and waited for Emmy to follow.

So she did. She felt funny about it, but by then her interest was aroused, and that made her ignore her natural reticence and follow Aiden from the truck to the house.

He did knock on the door but when there was no response he tried the handle and, sure enough, it turned easily and the door swung open with the mild complaint of rusty hinges.

A flip of the switch next to the door provided illumination from a bare bulb in the center of the one room and for a moment Emmy merely looked around in amazement that a woman owned and occupied it.

Rustic was too kind a word for it.

There was a twin-size mattress on the unfinished wood floor in one corner and a ragged green sofa with torn cushions against another wall. The opposite wall held a small table and one chair, both of which looked as if they'd been crafted by an untalented carpenter. And as for amenities, there was a chipped porcelain sink that looked more like a trough, a woodburning stove for cooking, a dorm-room-size refrigerator, and a bathtub and toilet all lined up in a row, without even a curtain to pull around the tub or toilet for privacy.

"She left a note," Aiden said, picking up a sheet of white paper from the table.

"What does it say?" Emmy asked when he'd had the chance to look at it.

"That she went fishing upriver."

"And that's it? Nothing else?"

"Nothing else. But then that's her style," Aiden said.

"Style?" Emmy repeated as she continued to scan what most people would consider a horribly deprived existence, not style.

"Nora is…" Aiden didn't seem to have a ready description of the other woman. "…a rugged individualist?" he finally said, still sounding unsure if that described her. "She's not someone who wants to deal with a lot of material things."

"A baby isn't a material thing, but it would be hard to have one here," Emmy commented.

Then she glanced around a second time, looking for any signs that there might have ever been an infant on the premises.

"There aren't any baby things," she concluded. "Not even a crib."

Aiden was doing a search of his own, opening the small cupboard where foodstuffs, towels and blankets were stored. "There's no baby food or diapers, either. But that doesn't necessarily mean anything. Knowing

Nora she'd keep the accessories and the necessities to a minimum and she could have just packed everything there was and brought it with Mickey.''

If Emmy hadn't seen for herself the conditions under which Nora Finley lived she might have thought that impossible. But now it wasn't so far-fetched.

''I'm trying to picture this woman,'' Emmy said more to herself than to Aiden.

But he heard her, anyway, and said, ''She's not a fashion plate. In fact, she doesn't even own a mirror. She's...'' Again he was at a loss for words and he eventually settled on ''...stocky.''

''Stocky?'' Emmy parroted.

''Not fat. But solid. Like a man. She wears her hair like a man, too—she has it cut at the barber shop. And I've never seen her in anything but men's clothes, men's boots, a man's coat. She can hunt and fish and trap with the best of them. And she can also drink us all under the table if she's so inclined. She's...well, I doubt that she's like anyone you know.''

''And you slept with her?'' The question came out of Emmy's mouth unfiltered.

''I didn't think I had, no,'' he confessed.

He stopped looking around to face Emmy, and his expression made her think he was having as much trouble believing it as she was.

Then he said, ''There have been two points in my life when I was so low I was looking up at hell— when I was a kid and both my parents were killed in a car accident and the day my wife left me. I know it was stupid, but when Rebecca walked out I didn't want to be alone and I went into town, to the inn, and tied one on.''

"Your *wife?* You were married? I didn't know…'' Emmy blurted out in surprise. Then, afraid he was telling her this because he thought he had to for the sake of the grant, when that wasn't the case—not to mention that it also wasn't any of her business—she said, "You don't have to explain.''

"It's okay,'' he assured her. "Yes, I was married. Once upon a time. Only that's not the point. The point is, I'm not proud of getting drunk or of what might have happened under the influence. I just want you to understand that I'm not some kind of sleaze.''

"I don't think you're a sleaze.''

But still he insisted on telling her the whole story, anyway.

"I drank more than I ever had in my life that night. Nora happened to be there—along with a lot of other people. But one by one everybody else had enough and went home, and then it was just Nora and me. I don't even remember leaving the bar, but when Nora comes to town she's always looking for someone to put her up for a night or two, so when I woke up the next morning and found a note from her, I figured I'd just given her a place to crash.''

"What did *that* note say?'' Emmy knew that was absolutely none of her business, but he'd already opted for telling her this stuff so she felt more free to indulge her curiosity.

"It said, 'Thanks for a good time.'''

Emmy's eyebrows rose all on their own. "And that didn't make you wonder if it applied to more than drinking?"

"It might have, except I still had on the pants I'd worn the night before. And the boots."

He admitted that almost reluctantly. Maybe because if he had made love to Nora Finley that night it didn't portray him as much of a Casanova to have done it without even removing his pants and boots.

"And if Mickey is yours and Nora's, that would be the night he was conceived," Emmy finished for him.

"It's the only possibility," Aiden confirmed.

Emmy wasn't too sure what to say then. She was pleased to know the truth about what had happened, to have him confide in her. But she didn't have any idea what the correct response to something like that was.

So she opted for levity.

"Well, if Mickey is yours, don't ever tell him that story."

It took a moment for that advice to sink in, and when it did Aiden's tense features relaxed into a smile.

"No, I don't think I will," he agreed with a laugh.

There didn't seem to be a reason to stay any longer, and after glancing around one last time, Aiden said, "While we're here, let me leave Nora a note so if she comes back without hearing the radio announcements she'll still call me. Then we can go." Aiden paused a moment, during which his light-blue eyes warmed her from the inside out. "And thanks," he added.

"For what?"

"For not making me feel any worse than I already do."

Aiden wasn't very talkative throughout the remainder of the trip back to his cabin where his nurse, Maria, had already brought Mickey home and put him to sleep for the night.

Emmy didn't mind that Aiden needed a little quiet, contemplative time, but he seemed to feel guilty about it, because once they'd said good-night to Maria he turned to Emmy and apologized, "I'm sorry I've been so uncommunicative. How about I make it up to you with a pizza and a beer?"

They'd been offered a variety of snacks through their travels but they hadn't actually had a meal since breakfast, and Emmy was starved. "Sounds good. Do you have pizza delivery in Boonesbury?"

"No," he said with a laugh. "There's a take-out pizza place in town that's closed by now. I keep a couple of their pies in the freezer for nights like tonight when I work late and come home hungry. It doesn't take long to reheat one of them, and they're better than store-bought frozen pizzas."

"Okay, I'm game."

"Why don't you go up and turn on the space heater while I put the pizza in the oven? After you left last night it occurred to me that we'd forgotten to do that."

So he'd been thinking about her even after she was gone....

Knowing that gave Emmy a secret satisfaction.

But still the suggestion that she go upstairs was a good one. Not only for the sake of having heat when she went to bed later on. She also wanted to freshen up just a bit. So she assured Aiden she'd only be a minute and headed for the attic room.

When she got there Emmy didn't change clothes—that would have been too obvious. But she did run a brush through her hair, apply more blush and find a slightly darker shade of lipstick to wear.

Then, after some debate during which she reminded herself that it was uncalled for, she added just a hint of perfume, anyway. Not as much as she might have used for a night on the town, but not as little as she might have dabbed on for a workday.

She worried about the impression she might be giving as she descended the steps to the lower level a few minutes later, but when she got back inside the main portion of the cabin those worries flew out the window.

Aiden had done some sprucing up himself—his five-o'clock shadow was history and he'd rejuvenated his aftershave.

It was okay, she assured herself. As long as she kept things in perspective and remembered that even though she enjoyed the man's company, this was still business—or so she kept telling herself—not pleasure.

Aiden was right about the pizza—it was better than

anything she'd tried from the grocery store's freezer case. And his choice of beer to go with it came from a small brewery in Anchorage and was just the right complement.

But still Aiden seemed slightly on the quiet side and Emmy decided to take the burden of conversation upon herself.

"You said you were just a kid when your parents were killed," she said, referring to what he'd told her earlier in Nora Finley's cabin. "How old were you?"

"I was nine. My brothers—Ethan and Devon— were ten and eight."

"I didn't know you had brothers. So there were three of you? Left without parents? How awful."

"Goes without saying."

"Who raised you all after that?" Emmy asked.

Aiden smiled again, this one sort of soft and nostalgic. "The small town of Dunbar, Colorado."

"You were raised by a *town?* You're going to have to explain that one," Emmy said with a laugh of her own.

"My brothers and I didn't have any relatives, and the good citizens of Dunbar—where we'd always lived—didn't want us to be put into foster homes or risk losing each other, which is what would most likely have happened to us. But it wasn't a rich community then, and no one family alone could afford three extra kids, so the folks there got together and pitched in. There was a fund established by the town to provide for us, and we spent time with everybody."

"Is that a kind way of saying you were passed around?"

"It didn't feel like that," Aiden assured. "It was handled so well that we just felt like everyone wanted us."

"How did it work? One brother at one house and another somewhere else? For a week or a month, or what?"

"No, they kept us together—well, until we got to be teenagers and we wanted to spend more time with our respective friends. But for the most part we were at the same houses at the same times. The length of time we stayed varied—a month, two, maybe three. Then someone else would come around, ask us if we might like to stay with them for a while, and we'd go."

"What if you didn't want to go?"

"Usually there was a lure that made us want to— new kittens or cable TV or something. I'm sure it was all arranged behind our backs, but, like I said, it was handled in a way that we felt like the most wanted kids in town."

"That sounds nice but wasn't it confusing? Living with a succession of different people? In different places? With different routines? Different rules?"

"It really wasn't so bad. Everybody knew everybody else and one household was pretty much like another. And there were benefits—great fried chicken at one place, a basketball hoop and a trampoline at another, pets here and there. In fact, one of the families we stayed with was the Briscoes—Dr. B. and his wife and daughter. Dr. B. ended up being my mentor—the whole reason I went to medical school. He treated each of us like the sons he never had, and when I showed an interest in medicine he took me, in particular, under his wing. If I hadn't spent so much time with him, I might not be a doctor today.''

Emmy had finished eating and had settled into just watching Aiden as he talked. She kept reminding herself of what she'd thought coming down from the attic room—that this was basically a business dinner during which she could further interview the person who would oversee the use of the grant money.

But it was difficult to believe the evening wasn't far more personal. After all, she'd never had a business dinner with Howard that had left her so aware of every detail of him, every nuance. Never had she even noticed the curve of Howard's lips when he smiled. Or even what color Howard's eyes were, let alone whether or not they seemed able to penetrate hers. Never had she been aware of what Howard's jaw did when he chewed—or thought it was sexy. And certainly she'd never watched Howard's hand curve around a bottle of beer and marveled at how adept it was or thought that she wished it was on her instead....

Business. This is business, she told herself sternly, forcing her thoughts back to the subject.

Or at least to an offshoot of the subject so she could pretend she was interviewing him. For the grant.

"So if your growing-up years in this Dunbar place were good, why come to Alaska to practice?" she asked. "I'd have thought you would have stayed in Colorado. Maybe to work with your Dr. B."

"That was my original plan. But Dunbar grew some when my brother Ethan brought his software headquarters there. Dr. B. found himself in need of help with the increased patient load. I had finished my residency but there were still a few years I owed the military because they'd paid for med school."

"And you couldn't pay the government back in Dunbar," Emmy guessed.

"There isn't a military base in Dunbar. I was stationed in Alaska, and Dr. B. took on someone else as a partner. Then, before my stint was up, Dr. B. had a heart attack and was forced to retire, and his partner brought in someone else."

"Couldn't you have gone there and started your own practice?"

"I could have. But even with the bigger population, Dunbar didn't need three doctors. So, I liked it here, liked the diversity of the people and cultures, liked the small-town, country-doctor thing, and I was needed. I decided to stay."

Aiden had stopped eating by this time, and he pushed his chair back onto two legs the way every mother warns her child not to. He raised his arms, clasping his hands behind his handsome head in a way that made it seem as if he'd finally shed the stress that had originated in Nora Finley's cabin.

"So there you have it—Aiden Tarlington, the early years. Pretty exciting stuff, huh?"

Excited was just what Emmy was feeling, but it

didn't have much to do with the story of his childhood. Her excitement came from the pure animal magnetism of the storyteller.

And realizing that was Emmy's cue to leave.

"We'd better clean up and call it a night," she said then.

"Why better we?"

Emmy laughed at the silliness of that response. "Is that a sentence?"

"Okay, why *should* we?" he amended with a mischievous challenge in his voice.

It wasn't easy, but Emmy resisted being drawn into the teasing, flirting tone. "We should clean up and call it a night because it's getting late and we had a long day." Then, as if that settled the matter, she stood and gathered the paper plates they'd used as dinnerware and said, "What's on tomorrow's agenda?"

Aiden didn't budge. He merely watched her as he answered. "Office hours in the a.m. Hygiene, nutrition, and no-smoking lectures at the school in the afternoon. Not much to rest up for."

Did he not want to end the evening?

The very thought made something like delight skitter through her.

Which was exactly why she knew she had to go.

"I still think it's time I get upstairs."

Aiden lowered his arms and let the chair fall back onto all four legs, sighing with resignation as he did. "Okay. You're the boss," he said, sounding as if he didn't agree with her dictate even though he knew he should go along with it.

Not that Emmy was entirely in favor of it herself. She really wanted to be right where she was. She wanted to go on talking to him. Looking at him. Learning about him.

Which was yet one more reason why she must not stay.

Aiden grabbed their empty beer bottles and together they took the entire remnants of their meal to the trashcan Aiden had under the sink.

Emmy led the way, reaching it first to drop what she'd brought into the plastic-lined can.

Then Aiden bent over from behind her to do the same.

He was close enough for his chest to brush her shoulder.

Had he been any other man, Emmy might have been incensed. She might have been uncomfortable. She might have ducked away and given him quite a dressing down.

But this was Aiden.

Aiden, with the incredible body that she never seemed to tire of looking at.

Aiden, with that carefree hair and that perfectly angular face.

Aiden, with those hands she was still yearning to have touch her.

Aiden, who had such a potent appeal that it was virtually impossible to ignore, let alone resist.

So Emmy wasn't incensed. She wasn't uncomfortable. And she certainly wasn't thinking about ducking away.

She was thinking about leaning back against him. About resting her head on his chest and having those long arms of his wrap around her...

Then he dropped the beer bottles into the trash and stepped back.

Probably because his coming into contact with her had only been an accident.

Emmy couldn't believe all that had gone through her mind in what was essentially only a fleeting moment.

It was definitely time for her to leave, she thought. Time to put some distance between them so she could once again regroup and shore up her defenses to this raging attraction.

But when she turned from the sink with every intention of making a beeline for the door, Aiden was still too close.

He was standing only a scant few feet away and Emmy nearly met him nose to chest before she came up short.

He didn't move, though. He held his ground, looking down at her, studying her.

"Did I thank you for today at Nora's place?" he said, his voice suddenly quiet and intimate.

"You did," Emmy assured over the pounding of her pulse as that excitement she'd felt before increased tenfold.

"Well, thanks for tonight, too. I was feeling...I don't know, kind of discouraged about all this stuff with Mickey and maybe Nora. But you lured me out of the doldrums.''

"I didn't do anything.''

"You provided a worthy distraction.''

"Worthy?'' she repeated with a laugh, to make light of what he was attributing to her.

"Okay, how about a pleasant distraction?''

"Pleasant is good,'' she conceded. "I really don't think I did anything, though.''

Aiden leaned in closer and, in a confidential—and very sexy—whisper, he said, "When someone is thanking you for something, just say 'You're welcome.'''

"You're welcome,'' Emmy repeated, mimicking him, even as she was trying not to like the smell of his aftershave so much. Or the feel of the heat of his skin when he got that close.

He straightened up again, but it didn't seem as if he was as far back as he'd been before.

Not that Emmy minded; she just knew she should have.

And he didn't seem to have anything else to say, either, because he merely let his striking baby-blue eyes meet hers, holding them in a warmth that seeped in through her pores.

Then he leaned forward again and kissed her. Only once. Lightly. Chastely. Sweetly. And in a shorter time than Emmy would have chosen, it was over.

From the look on Aiden's face, he'd surprised himself as much as he'd surprised her.

"Oh-oh. Who was that masked man?" he joked, sounding uneasy with what he'd just done.

"The Lone Ranger?" Emmy said, off-balance herself and opting to play along to conceal it.

Another moment elapsed as they went on studying each other. Before Aiden took a deep breath, blew it out and admitted, "I don't know what got into me. If you want to slap me or something, go ahead."

"I don't want to slap you," Emmy assured him.

On the contrary, she wanted him to kiss her again. Slower this time. Longer. So maybe she would have the chance to do more in the way of kissing him back....

But of course she couldn't say that.

Instead she said, "It's okay."

"Maybe you're right and it has been a long day."

"It has," she agreed.

"And I was having a good time and I lost sight of—"

"Right, of the fact that this is business," Emmy supplied.

"Right. Business," Aiden confirmed. "It just doesn't feel like business," he added, somewhat under his breath and more to himself than to her.

Emmy didn't address that. She was too afraid of where agreeing with him—because she *did* agree with him—might lead.

"I should go upstairs," she said. But somehow there was a note of question to it.

"Probably should," Aiden said, not sounding any more convinced than she did.

But thoughts of Howard and the foundation and the grant and the fact that she truly was only there on business finally caused Emmy to tear her eyes away from Aiden's, to step around him and head for the door.

"Eight tomorrow morning?" she said when she'd reached it, holding on to the handle as if it were her lifeline as she cast a glance over her shoulder at him.

"Sure," he said.

Only then did he turn to look at her, falling back to lean his hips against the edge of the counter and folding his arms over his broad chest.

Once again their eyes met and held, and even from that distance Emmy could feel the power in those eyes of his. The power to mesmerize her.

And she couldn't help thinking how much she wanted him to cross the cabin to her.

To kiss her again.

But he didn't do that. He didn't move so much as one glorious muscle.

And it was just as well that he didn't.

Because if he had, Emmy wasn't too sure she could have made herself actually say good night to him, open that door and walk through it the way she finally did a moment later.

And all from a single, simple kiss.

A single, simple kiss that had still managed to make her heart race....

Chapter Five

"All right, Mickey my boy, here we are—the start of a new day. How do you feel about a delectable dish of baby cereal?" Aiden said to his young charge as he sat at the kitchen table where Mickey was perched in his car seat.

Mickey blew spit bubbles in answer and then became very pleased with himself for the accomplishment.

"A new day," Aiden repeated with the first spoonful he fed the infant. "And I'm going to try my damnedest not to do anything stupid with our lady friend from upstairs."

A second bite was delivered and accepted.

"Yeah, I couldn't believe it myself when I kissed her last night," Aiden said as if they were in the middle of a conversation. "*Kissed* her, for crying out loud. And then there I was, looking at her shocked face and wondering what I'd done. Kissing the one woman who's here to judge whether we can have money we need for these folks' medical care? Bad move. Really bad move."

Mickey didn't seem to think so because he gave Aiden a cereal-laced grin.

"What if she starts thinking I'm coming on to her to get the money?" Aiden argued. "What if she doesn't realize that the one has nothing to do with the other? Because it doesn't. She just has this smile that's as warm as the first sunshine after a long winter. And eyes that have me losing my train of thought every time I look into them. And it doesn't help that I have more fun with her than I've had in too long to remember. Or that I never know what she's going to say next. Or that she makes me laugh...."

Mickey made a guttural sound as if to keep up his side of the chat.

And, as if Aiden had understood it, he said, "Sure, if the situation were different I might go for it. But the situation isn't different. She's up here for business—as she reminded me after that dumb move I made last night. Important business. And kissing her? That was as bad as kissing one of my board examiners. So why the hell was I kissing her?"

Aiden wiped Mickey's chin before giving the baby the next bite.

"It's not going to happen again, I can tell you that. I don't care how cute she is or how much I like her or how great a time I'm having with her. There's too much at stake. And not just for Boonesbury,'' he added under his breath.

Then, as if Mickey had prodded him, he admitted, ''Yeah, that's right. Rebecca. No way I'm letting myself in for that kind of fall again. Stick with women who already live in Alaska so they know what they're in for—that's what I swore I was going to do. And I meant it.''

Mickey seemed enthralled with Aiden and his monologue as he continued to eat his breakfast.

''There are plenty of good women up here. Well, maybe not plenty, but enough. I spend time with Shelly when she comes through town to do dental work every three months or so. And Cindy, the pharmaceutical rep. She was born in Anchorage. She lives in Fairbanks. I see her at least once a month and it could be more often if I wanted it to be.''

Mickey tried blowing another bubble, but this time it was with cereal in his mouth and Aiden barely missed being sprayed with it.

''Okay, so what if I'm never obsessed with seeing them the way I've been obsessed with seeing Emmy every day since she's been here? So what if I never watched the clock or listened for them or wished they would hurry up and get here the way I have over her every morning this week? At least when they are here I'm not worrying about how much they hate the life I lead. I'm not worrying that they can't wait to get back to the lower forty-eight and put as much distance as possible between themselves and me and Alaska.

They've made their homes here and so have I—that's a big thing to have in common. And I sure as hell don't have it in common with Emmy.''

Aiden fed Mickey another mouthful that ended up dribbled down the baby's chin rather than swallowed. Aiden got the hint—Mickey was full. So he set the bowl on the table and washed the infant's face.

''What am I, anyway? A glutton for punishment? Why *can't* I be dying to see Shelly or Cindy? No, I have to be sniffing after Emmy Harris, who would rather have her tonsils taken out than be in Alaska. Who's only here to see if we pass muster for grant money and who can nix our chances for it if I rub her wrong.''

Aiden dried the baby's face and then put baby and carrier on the floor where Mickey would be safe while he went to wash the cereal bowl.

''So what do you think? *Did* my kissing her rub her wrong?'' Aiden asked as if Mickey had the inside scoop. ''She didn't slap me—even when I offered to let her. Or ask what the hell I thought I was doing. But she did leave in a hurry. She ran like a rabbit. That can't be a good sign.''

He left the bowl and spoon on the drain board, returning to Mickey and taking him out of the car seat so he could move him into the bedroom for phase two of the morning ablutions.

''I know. I have to fight what's going on with Emmy. I can't give in to it. I have to curb these crazy impulses to touch her. To hold her. To kiss her. To… Nah, you're too young to hear what else I'd like to be doing with her. But take my word for it, I can't do it. I have to behave myself. For Boonesbury's sake and for my own. And for yours, too, if you and I prove to be more than pals.''

Aiden laid Mickey on the bed and unsnapped his pajamas.

"But it isn't easy, let me tell you. Because just between you and me, there's something about this woman…''

Mickey waved his arms and legs in a joyous response to nakedness. But Aiden acted as if the baby had just been the voice of reason.

"Yeah, you're right, there absolutely can't be any more kissing. No matter what there is about her. Or how bad I want to.''

And he wanted to so badly that for a moment he couldn't even talk about it. For a moment he struggled to find strength from somewhere deep inside to assure himself that he could resist whatever it was that drew him to Emmy with such power.

He finally found that strength in remembering his ex-wife. And what he'd gone through when his marriage had ended. In the reawakening of resolves he'd made then.

But even with that renewed strength to resist Emmy, even with the absolute knowledge that he never should have kissed Emmy, he still wasn't too sure he would actually be able to fight off the urge to kiss her again.

Because although kissing her once might have been

a mistake, he still wasn't convinced it wasn't a mistake worth repeating....

Emmy didn't know what the new day was going to bring. Or how she should act with Aiden after what had happened at the end of the evening before.

Of all the things her predecessor had complained about, having the representative of a grant's recipients kiss her was not on the list.

But then, if the representative of a grant's recipients had looked like Aiden, had been as charming, as charismatic, as appealing as Aiden, maybe Evelyn would have kept being kissed by him a secret. Certainly Emmy had no intention of filing a formal grievance.

Even though she'd been telling herself all night long and every minute since she'd been awake this morning how inappropriate the whole thing was. How inappropriate it was that Aiden had kissed her. And how more inappropriate it was that the only thing she actually found fault with about it was the brief duration of that kiss.

Of all the unprofessional things she'd thought and felt since setting eyes on the man, this was the worst yet, and even if the foundation's director's handbook didn't address a situation like this specifically, she was reasonably sure kissing one of the people she was interviewing for a grant was against the rules.

Although technically, she *hadn't* kissed Aiden. He'd kissed her. So she hadn't stepped out of line yet.

It was just that she wanted to.

Well, she didn't want to step out of line.

But, oh, brother, did she want him to kiss her again so she could kiss him back!

She was reluctant to admit that even to herself. But as she dressed in a pair of gray slacks and a charcoal-gray turtleneck sweater, she knew she would be lying to say she *didn't* want an elaborate repeat of the event.

But what she wanted and what she intended to do were two different things. Which was really what made seeing him again feel awkward. And complicated.

Because no matter how much she would have liked to let the personal side of things evolve with the man, she just couldn't do it. She just wouldn't do it.

Emmy brushed her hair and twisted it into a knot at the back of her head that left a spray of spiky ends at her crown.

As she did she wondered if she should confront Aiden. If she should explain that she wasn't upset by what had happened but that it couldn't happen again.

"That *would* be awkward," she told her reflection in the mirror as she considered it.

Awkward and embarrassing for them both.

Not to mention that it would probably put a very sour note on the remainder of this trip, which was something Emmy wasn't in favor of, either. For business reasons, making the rest of this visit stilted and uncomfortable for them both did not seem like the best way to accomplish what she'd come to accomplish.

So maybe it was just better to go on as if that kiss

had never happened. Maybe it was better to hope that rushing out the way she had the night before had given Aiden enough of a message to prevent it from happening again.

Besides, he'd seemed to be aware of the fact that he shouldn't have done it. He probably wouldn't do it again, anyway.

Which made it all a moot point and she could likely relax. The kiss had been a brief lapse and there wouldn't be another.

So why was she feeling disappointed at that thought?

"Cut it out," she ordered herself.

It didn't help. The disappointment remained.

But what she felt, what she wanted, what she was disappointed about wasn't important, she told herself as she applied mascara, blush and a light-colored lipstick. The only thing that *was* important was that she not act on any of them. That she keep everything contained and under control. That she practice self-restraint.

And that was exactly what she intended to do.

She intended to put professionalism and self-restraint into action and keep the feelings, the cravings, the disappointment contained until they dried up and disappeared.

Which was what they would do eventually, wouldn't they?

Of course they would.

And in the long run, she and Aiden and all of Boonesbury would be better off for it.

"Good to have that settled," she said as she took one last glance at herself in the mirror and decided she was ready to go.

It was just that, as she grabbed her coat, the new day suddenly seemed a little duller.

And she was looking forward to it a whole lot less.

Aiden's "Come in," in answer to Emmy's knock on the front door a few minutes later, was enough to send tiny shivers of delight up her spine.

But she kept her goals in mind, straightened her shoulders and didn't allow herself to get out of the cold until she was convinced she could keep her eye on the ball.

Then she opened the door and let herself in.

"It's just me," she announced as she did.

Aiden was nowhere in sight, but from what sounded like his bedroom, he added, "I'll be right out. Mickey just anointed my shirt. I have to change into a clean one."

So, only a few feet away, Aiden was bare-chested....

Emmy's mouth went dry as she imagined how wonderful he must look without a shirt on. Broad, naked shoulders. Hard pectorals. A flat, washboard stomach.

Did he have hair on his chest? she wondered. A little? A lot?

"No rush," she answered, somewhat belatedly and in a voice that cracked slightly. But she chanted silently, *Professionalism and self-restraint. Profession-*

alism and self-restraint. And that helped chase the uninvited images out of her brain. Sort of.

Mickey was lying on a blanket in the middle of the living room floor, and Emmy went to him, seizing the likeliest distraction to help keep her resolve.

The baby's response to her as she came into his line of vision helped. Mickey seemed to recognize her. He grinned and gurgled a hello.

"Good morning," Emmy greeted him.

Ignoring her original vow not to get involved in anything other than grant-connected affairs, Emmy bent over and picked up the infant.

She paid for it with a flash of memory that, once upon a time, when she'd had a Grand Plan, this particular year was to have been the year she had a baby of her own.

But the twinge of residual emotional pain that came with the realization at least helped keep her from thinking about a bare-torsoed Aiden in the next room.

She sat on the sofa with Mickey and laid him in her lap—his head braced against her knees—so she could take his hands in hers and play with him.

He really was an adorable baby. His eyes were big and round, and as dark as twin chips of bittersweet chocolate. His cheeks were so chubby she just wanted to nuzzle them. And those two tiny teeth that poked through his bottom gums gave him irresistible character.

Emmy only got to play with him for a moment, though, before Aiden appeared in the archway that led to the bedrooms.

"Hi," he said, sounding glad to see her.

"Morning," Emmy responded, looking up from Mickey to find Aiden freshly shaved and dressed in a pair of brown corduroy pants and a dress shirt the same color.

But the shirt wasn't open down the front the way she'd half hoped it might be so she could get a glimpse of that chest she'd been fantasizing about. The shirt was completely buttoned and tucked in, and Aiden was knotting a brown and blue tie over it.

"There's the usual stuff for breakfast," he offered amiably enough.

If the kiss was still on his mind, the way it was on hers, he didn't show it. And that fact gave Emmy new impetus to submerge those thoughts that still lingered in spite of everything she'd done to chase them away.

"No, thanks, I'm not hungry," she said, when the truth was her stomach was too jittery to put anything into.

"Maria will have coffee and donuts at the office if you want something later."

Emmy just nodded and returned her gaze to Mickey, making silly faces to entertain him.

Aiden finished tying his tie and came the rest of the way into the living room then to sit on the edge of the overstuffed chair just to her left.

"Better get our boy into his snowsuit," he said, holding out his hands for Emmy to pass Mickey to him.

She did and as Aiden began to dress the infant, he said, "Look, about last night..."

Emmy felt her stress level rise, and she stood to put on her coat, too, just to give herself something to do as Aiden continued.

"I just want you to know it was no big deal. I'm sure it was purely a spontaneous thing, and while I can't say I have a lot of women kissing me out of the blue, I kind of liked it when you did."

Emmy turned her head to stare at him.

He'd said that with a perfectly straight face.

The joke caught her off guard but when she realized it *was* a joke, she couldn't help laughing.

"Is that right?" she said facetiously.

"I confess that I was a little taken aback by it but then my main man Mickey here said, 'Aiden, just chill out. Count yourself lucky that a beautiful woman got momentarily carried away and leave it at that.'"

Emmy glanced at Mickey who was sucking his fist. "Did you say that?" she asked, playing along.

"He's a wise kid. He also pointed out that there was that one beer you had. You weren't in complete command of your faculties—after all, we know what alcoholic beverages can do to a person's inhibitions. So we decided it was probably best to just let this one slide," Aiden teased.

"Thank you. I really appreciate your forbearance."

"Anytime."

"Does that mean I can go ahead and kiss you anytime, or that you're willing to excuse me anytime I do?" she asked, sticking with the joke.

"Both. Of course in the future—"

"Oh, no, never mind. In the future I'll just make sure to completely keep my hands off you."

Aiden made a face. "Now that might be going a little too far."

Emmy laughed again. "You know, I think maybe you're evil."

"Shh—don't go giving away all my secrets. I understand there's a woman around here checking me out for a grant of some kind. She could get the wrong idea."

He was grinning at her now, enjoying this. And unless she was mistaken, he didn't feel too much regret about the way he'd ended the evening before.

But for some reason Emmy didn't want to analyze, it pleased her that he didn't seem terribly sorry he'd kissed her.

"Oh, I don't think the woman checking you out will get the wrong idea," she assured him, liking all the ideas she had about him. Liking him, too. More than she wished she did.

"Guess we better get to work, though, before she starts thinking I'm a slacker."

"Guess so."

If defusing tension had been his intention, he'd succeeded.

Although it did occur to her that their being comfortable with each other was what had gotten them into trouble in the first place, and that maybe some stress would have helped maintain those boundaries she still hadn't really set and probably should have.

But the relief she was experiencing felt too good to willingly give up.

Just like being with him did.

So Emmy let everything else go and merely held the door open for him to carry Mickey and the car seat outside.

They listened to the radio on the drive to Aiden's office, hearing the announcement about Mickey once more and the plea for Nora Finley to call Aiden.

The topic of Mickey seemed to have gained rather than lost interest. There were several calls to the DJ offering comments about the abandoned baby and help with his care—if Aiden needed it. There were also a few sly, teasing remarks made as an increasing number of people seemed to be putting two and two together when it came to Aiden and Nora Finley.

The office waiting room was packed by the time they arrived, and following Aiden through his paces again gave Emmy more of an indication of where the grant money would be used and why it was needed.

Maria, who Emmy learned was not actually a nurse but trained only as a medical technician, had more duties and more work than she should have had, and Emmy concluded that the practice would benefit by the addition of a registered nurse—something the grant could provide for.

As with the other day at the office, Mickey was passed around and played with, although those patients who thought they might be contagious steered clear of the infant.

Lunch consisted of stolen bites of sandwiches between appointments, and Aiden barely finished seeing the morning round of patients in time for them to rush to the school.

Elementary, middle school, and high school classes were all held in the same building. One room for each section was all that was needed since there were only two or three students in any grade.

Aiden visited each one, concentrating on good nutrition and the importance of hygiene with the youngest kids, adding the no-smoking warnings with the middle school, and the no-smoking plus a talk about safe sex with the high schoolers who joked with him as if he were their older brother.

Emmy added a need for visual aids to her list of things the grant money might supply. Then it was back to the office for more appointments, and finally home again well after dark.

And that was what Aiden had referred to the night before as a light day.

Mickey had stayed with Maria to nap while Emmy and Aiden had gone to the school, but he still seemed worn-out when they got him to the cabin. He was half-asleep through his dinner and bath, and out like a light the moment Aiden put him in his crib.

Aiden fixed a Southwestern casserole for himself and Emmy to share, and while they ate they went over the notes she'd taken during the day. Aiden had only one addition to make. He suggested she add flu and pneumonia vaccines, because if Boonesbury was awarded the grant he wanted to use some of the money to offset the cost so his lower-income patients would be more apt to get the shots every year.

Then the meal was finished and the dishes were done, and Aiden said, "Okay, the workday is officially over. How do you feel about home movies? Or more precisely, about watching a video of my brother's wedding?"

"I like weddings," Emmy answered. And she *didn't* like the thought of saying good-night and going upstairs to the attic room. Despite the fact that she'd been with Aiden since early that morning, it still didn't seem as if she'd had enough time with him yet.

"Which brother got married?" she asked as they relocated to the living room.

"Ethan—my older brother."

"When?"

"About two weeks ago."

Aiden was turning on the television and putting the tape into the VCR, and it was almost impossible not to look at his back view as he did. It was right there. Directly in front of her as she sat on the couch.

Not that she minded. He had a body made for admiring, and the corduroys he was wearing had just enough hug to accentuate the great derriere they caressed.

It was just that she knew she *shouldn't* be admiring it. Or ogling it. Or wanting to caress it herself—so much so that her palms actually tingled and she tried counteracting it by pressing them to her knees.

But what she didn't do was look away.

Then Aiden turned around, and staring at the flip side was even less appropriate.

Her pulse picked up speed, and more than her palms tingled to life.

But this time she did force her gaze away, yanking it to his handsome face as he joined her on the sofa.

There was limited space from which the TV could be seen, and so they ended up sitting side by side at one end of the couch.

Side by side and so close together Emmy could feel the heat of his big body and smell the lingering, enticing scent of his aftershave.

And what she wanted to do was lean into him, put her head on his shoulder, snuggle up with him to watch the recording of his brother's wedding.

She didn't do any of that, but she did find herself relaxing her muscles enough so that her thigh barely rested against the thick, solid length of his.

An instant flash of guilt ran through her for the indulgence, but even barely touching him felt too nice and she couldn't bring herself to pull away.

She did work to get her mind back to more acceptable things, though.

"Were you at the wedding?" she asked, imagining Aiden all dressed up and how terrific he would look.

But he dashed her hopes for seeing him like that. "No, I couldn't make it. I had a patient I couldn't leave."

"You got stuck here on an emergency?" Emmy probed.

Her impression had been that he was close to his

brothers in spite of the fact that they were separated by distance, and she would have expected Aiden to make it to one of those brothers' weddings no matter what.

"It wasn't an emergency, no," Aiden answered. "My patient was dying. There was nothing I could do for her—she was very old and she just started to fail. But she didn't have any family or friends left and I didn't want to leave her alone in the hospital with a bunch of strangers."

"So you missed your brother's wedding to sit with her until she died?"

"Mmm. But now we have the movie," he said as enthusiastically as an advertisement for a soon-to-be-released blockbuster.

It occurred to Emmy that if she ended up alone in the world when it came time for her to die, she hoped she had a doctor caring enough to miss his brother's wedding to sit with her. But she thought she might embarrass Aiden if she said that, so instead she let the subject drop and said, "Better give me background. Were your brother and his fiancée old high school sweethearts or merging moguls or was this a marriage of convenience? Set it up for me."

"It was a whirlwind romance. They met a while ago and spent one night together just before he left the country. He looked her up when he got back and discovered they had a baby daughter. Sparks flew a second time when they got reacquainted, and now they're going to live happily ever after. Or at least that's the hope, isn't it?"

"Is that an edge of cynicism I hear?" Emmy asked, surprised by it.

Aiden gave her a chagrined smile. "My own baggage. Ignore it. The truth is, I like Paris. I know my brother loves her. They have a beautiful little girl they're both crazy about, and I honestly do think it will work out for them."

And with that, he aimed the remote control and fired, effectively cutting short that portion of the conversation.

"The wedding was in Dunbar," Aiden informed her then, as the film began.

"That's the small town that raised you and your brothers," Emmy recalled, going with the flow of things.

"Right. This is Ethan's house there—"

"Wow! It's huge."

"Software has been very good to him. That's the backyard—it was a candlelit garden wedding."

The camera spanned the site, giving them a look at the decorations, the rows and rows of empty white chairs arranged like church pews, the latticed arch where the ceremony itself was to be performed. Then they were treated to a view into a giant tent where the wedding cake stood six tiers high, buffet tables were laden with mouthwatering delectables, and where dining tables, a dance floor and a bandstand waited for the reception.

"I can't believe how many red roses there were," Emmy said.

"And how many candles. I'm going to have to ask Ethan for the full count just to boggle my mind."

The tape switched to inside the house. Into what looked like a bedroom.

"Those two guys are my brothers," Aiden narrated.

The two men on-screen resembled Aiden so much Emmy would have realized that was who they were even without the commentary.

"Ethan is on the right—he's in the vest," Aiden continued. "Devon is on the left in the cummerbund."

Both of them were tall, well built, and strikingly handsome. But in Emmy's estimation, not quite as handsome as Aiden.

Up to that point there hadn't been any sound but now Aiden's brothers faced the camera and spoke.

"Hey, A," Devon said, obviously addressing Aiden. "You're missing out on all the fun. Big E is as nervous as he was in the fourth grade when he kissed Mary Ellen Montgomery for the first time. Remember that? Hit and run, and he was still so scared his teeth were clattering like he was freezing to death."

Beside Devon, Ethan rolled his eyes. "That's a lie. I'm not nervous at all."

"Took him three times to button the vest before he got it right," Devon said with a laugh. "I don't know how I'm going to hold him up without you here to help. I think he might faint."

"Don't make me flatten you on my wedding day," Ethan warned.

Devon only laughed. "No, seriously, can you believe he's taking the leap? Mr. All Work and No Play? And you should see him changing diapers. He's a pro. We could hire him out as a nanny."

"Wait till you see how big Hannah's gotten, Aiden," Ethan said, sounding like a proud papa.

"Tell him how much she likes me, though," Devon urged, the equally proud uncle.

"She dimples up for him every time he comes into the room," Ethan confirmed. "We're beginning to worry about her taste in men."

Devon didn't pay any attention to the gibe. "I'm carrying her down the aisle."

There was the sound of a door opening somewhere off camera and then a voice saying it was time for them to get outside.

Both men slipped into their tuxedo jackets and, contrary to Devon's teasing, Emmy didn't think Ethan seemed nervous at all. She thought he looked happy and eager to get on with the wedding.

Then, completely dressed for the occasion, the oldest Tarlington brother spoke to the camera again. "Wish you were here with us, A. Pretend you're standing up with me for this, okay?"

Then Aiden's brothers left the room, and the next part of the film was of the procession down the aisle.

"Hannah *has* gotten big," Aiden said about the beautiful baby girl his brother carried to the archway after the other groomsmen had escorted the bridesmaids ahead of them.

Paris Hanley was stunning in antique lace, and she

beamed at her groom as she joined him to face the minister.

The ceremony was solemn and touching, and as Emmy watched, she tried hard not to think about her own wedding. About her own hopes and dreams on that day and how they hadn't come to be. And she silently wished the other couple better luck than she'd had.

Then the groom kissed his bride, and what followed were clips of the reception that was really just a great big, elaborate party where everyone seemed to have a wonderful time eating and drinking and dancing until Aiden's brother and his new wife slipped away.

There was a little more footage on the reception as the guests dwindled, and then a slightly inebriated and obviously emotional Devon was alone with the camera.

"That's it, A. I ate your piece of cake and drank your share of the champagne but it wasn't as good as having you here. We missed you, bro. But you're a good man to do what you're doin' instead. We're proud of you. See you soon, huh?"

Devon waved and the tape came to an end.

"That was nice," Emmy said as Aiden clicked off the VCR and then the television.

"It was, wasn't it?" Aiden agreed.

He leaned forward to put the remote control on the coffee table and when he sat back again he was just as close beside Emmy as he'd been before. Even though he could have put some distance between them, now that they didn't need to both see the television.

Then he stretched an arm along the top of the sofa cushion just behind her head, and a warm rush flooded through her.

Still, she was determined not to give in to that continuing inclination to cozy up to him. Self-restraint, she reminded herself. Practice self-restraint....

In an effort to do that, she let her curiosity about Aiden's comment just before he'd started the video have its way.

"The baggage you mentioned earlier that keeps you from believing in happily ever after—was that from your own marriage not lasting?" she asked, getting right to the heart of it.

"I was just spouting off. But yeah, I suppose that's where that touch of negativity came from."

"How long were you married?"

"A little over four years," he said.

"And she left you. That's what you said in Nora's cabin, didn't you?"

Aiden smiled slightly at Emmy, and it seemed as if he was taking her inquiry in stride. "She left me."

"Why?"

"You said that day at Nora's place that I didn't have to tell you this stuff for the grant. Has that changed?" he asked, with a joking hint of suspicion in his voice.

"You said the workday was over. I'm just wondering."

From his expression he was considering the truth

in that. Then, as if he didn't mind answering her questions so long as they were soothing her own personal interest, he said, "Alaska was part of the problem. Part of the reason she gave for leaving me. But I think it was more the symptom than the disease."

"She wasn't from here?"

"Nope. She was from Colorado. She was a nurse. I met her when I was doing my residency. We got married two months before I finished."

"And then you had to go into the military."

"Right. Thanks for paying attention."

As if she could keep herself from hanging on his every word.

But Emmy didn't admit that. She just said, "Sure."

Then Aiden picked up the story where he'd left off.

"We spent some time apart while I went through basic training, but when I was stationed in Alaska Rebecca moved here."

"And she didn't like it?"

"It was tough for her to commit to liking or disliking much of anything. The reality was that no matter how hard I tried to get her to take a more active role in the choices we made, she refused. But that didn't necessarily mean she was happy with the choices *I* made."

"And living in Boonesbury fell into that category?"

"That's what I learned in the end. But that wasn't how it started out."

"How did it start out?" Emmy asked.

"When I was discharged from the army and it was

time to pick a place to live, I asked where she would choose if she could choose anywhere on earth. But her answer was to ask me the same thing—that was generally what she did, toss it back to me. And then I'd make the decision.''

"And you decided on Alaska."

"Like I said before, I liked it here. I asked her a million times if she was sure that was okay with her, and she kept saying whatever I wanted was fine. But then we moved to Boonesbury and it wasn't fine. Apparently. She didn't let me know along the way that she was unhappy here. Or that she was unhappy with me making all the choices for us both. But one of us had to, and she wouldn't. Then one day she told me she was too sick to go into the office with me—she was my nurse at the time—and when I got home that night she had all her stuff packed and said she was leaving me.''

Emmy's eyebrows arched. "That must have been a shock."

"Oh, yeah," he agreed wryly.

"Did she say why?"

"At first she said it was Alaska. She hated the cold. The extended days and nights at the extremes of the seasons. The isolation. Everything about it. I offered to pull up stakes and move—for all her indecisiveness I was in love with her and I would have done anything to save the marriage. But that was when the tune changed.''

"And it wasn't *only* Alaska she wanted out of?" Emmy surmised.

Aiden shook his head. "It definitely wasn't only Alaska. She said I'd been doing all her thinking for her, and she was tired of it. I argued that I'd wanted her to think for herself, to be an equal in the relationship, but that she just hadn't done it. By that point it didn't matter, though. She was convinced that the only way she would ever make her own decisions or have the life *she* wanted was to start over, alone."

There were a few red flags for Emmy in what he was saying, but she tried to remember Aiden was talking about his past, and that this had nothing to do with her.

"Sounds like a divorce was the one decision she *had* made," Emmy observed.

"Sad to say. She got in her car that night and left. That was the last I saw of her. From then on everything was lawyers and courts until the marriage was no more."

"And you ended up spending a night with Nora Finley over it."

He actually flinched at that. "Not my proudest moment."

"And now you're not too sure any marriage can work out?"

He smiled at her again. "One off-the-cuff comment and you're not going to let me live it down, are you? I still believe in marriage. I'd even do it again."

"Oh, brave man," Emmy teased. "I'll bet you have some things you're on the lookout for, though."

"Sure. In fact, in some ways Nora Finley does fit that bill," he said with a laugh. "She certainly thinks for herself—that's one of the prerequisites for 'Marriage—the Sequel.'"

"And she likes Alaska," Emmy contributed as if she were adding to the pros of Aiden considering Nora Finley for a prospective wife.

"That, too. But I don't really like having the john in the kitchen, and she doesn't seem to mind—that could be a problem."

"Your whole place is like a palace compared to hers. Maybe she could get used to the finer things in life."

"Not Nora. This luxury would only be an encumbrance to her. I'll probably have to keep looking for my next wife."

He'd added that last part with a half-sarcastic, half-lascivious tone and a long, pointed look into Emmy's eyes, making her laugh.

Aiden smiled and chuckled himself before changing the subject.

"What about you? You know my whole life story, and all I know about you is your work history."

"That's the most interesting thing about me."

"I doubt that." He took her left hand in his and pretended to study it. "No ring, so I'm assuming you're single."

Emmy tried to fight the little shards of light that ran up her arm just from his touch.

"I am absolutely single," she said, wondering at the emphasis she'd unintentionally put on it.

"Have you ever been married?"

"Six...no, eight times," she joked.

His turn to laugh. "Does that mean never?"

"No. I was married," she conceded. "Once."

And she didn't want to talk about it right then.

But Aiden persisted. "And..." he said to urge more information out of her.

"And would you look at the time?" she said in an effort to change the subject. "It's too late to get into *my* sordid past. I'm sure we have a jam-packed day in store for us tomorrow."

"Office hours and a preparation-for-childbirth class. Then the homecoming bonfire tomorrow night, if you're interested," he informed her, as if it didn't amount to much.

But he might as well have doubled the duties; Emmy's response would have been the same. "See? What did I tell you? Busy, busy, busy. We'd better get some sleep."

He hadn't taken those striking blue eyes off her for even a moment since asking about her former marital status. And since Emmy hadn't moved from that spot on the sofa despite her verbal attempt to flee, she was still there, basking in the heat of that stare.

"I get it. You don't want to talk about your marriage," Aiden said then.

"It *is* late," Emmy said by way of confirmation. "And we really should go to bed."

She hoped that hadn't sounded as suggestive to him as it had to her.

But his answering smile told her it had. "Are you hinting at something?"

Emmy laughed again, slightly embarrassed this

time. "Turning up the flame on the hot seat, are you?"

"Maybe just a little."

"Well stop it. All I'm *suggesting* is that I say good-night and go upstairs."

But neither of them moved then, either.

And Emmy wondered if she was imagining it or if his arm had come closer to actually being around her.

"Killjoy," he accused in a tone that made it more of an endearment.

"That's me," she agreed with a breathiness to her voice that she hadn't put there intentionally.

Yet, again they stayed where they were. Only, now Aiden raised the hand that had been on the back of the couch cushion to toy with the spiky ends of her hair as he went on looking into her face, studying it, liking what he saw—if his expression was any indication.

The air all around them seemed to have altered and infused itself with something very sensual. It couldn't have been called tension because Emmy wasn't feeling stressed. But there was undeniably something sensuous happening in the atmosphere.

And despite telling herself to resist it, the spell that was weaving itself around them was more powerful than all of her resolves rolled up together.

Aiden stopped fiddling with her hair to rub the back of her neck in a leisurely massage that dipped his finger inside the turtleneck collar of her sweater.

His touch felt so good Emmy nearly moaned. And although she managed not to, she did incline her head just enough to give him freer access and let him know she liked what he was doing.

Of course that movement also tilted her chin upward, too. Almost in invitation.

And even though it hadn't been, when Aiden pressed his lips to hers she didn't balk. How could she, when, deep down, kissing her again was what she'd wanted him to do ever since he'd stopped kissing her the night before.

Except, tonight's kiss hadn't caught her so much by surprise. And it didn't end as abruptly as it had begun, either. Tonight there was no hurry in him. Tonight he *really* kissed her.

His lips parted over hers, savoring the moment and giving her the opportunity to ease into kissing him in return. Into parting her own lips in what actually was an invitation now.

His hand went from her neck to cradle her head as he deepened the kiss even more. As mouths opened wider and his tongue came to introduce itself.

And if Emmy had had any doubts about Aiden's kissing talents the previous evening, those doubts wouldn't have been able to survive. He was good at it. Great at it, in fact. So great that her mind emptied of all thoughts but him and that kiss. So great that she lost herself in it. That she couldn't do anything but allow it to engulf her.

His tongue said hello to hers and began to court it, and with every moment their game went on, things inside Emmy grew even softer, more pliable. As if warm honey had been poured into her veins.

She let her head rest in his palm, trusting his support, as she raised a hand of her own to the side of his face and absorbed the pleasure of what she'd been longing for more than she'd allowed herself to realize.

His skin was smooth and masculine, and she reveled in the feel of it. In the opportunity to touch him. In yet another way to know him.

She could have gone on kissing him forever. Exploring all the textures of his skin, his beard, his firm jawline.

She *wanted* to go on kissing him forever and exploring that oh-so-incredible face.

But it was Aiden who stopped things.

Slowly.

By reluctant degrees.

But nevertheless he stopped that kiss that Emmy didn't think she would ever have been able to end herself.

"I did it again, didn't I?" he said in a voice raspy with the impact of what they'd just shared.

"Better than the last time," she said, making light of what had just happened.

"I guess I didn't get it all out of my system," he said with a crooked smile that held no more regrets for this kiss than he'd seemed to have for the previous one.

"Did you get it out of your system now?" she asked, peering up into his achingly handsome features.

Aiden laughed, a throaty, sexy sound. "No, I don't think you could say that."

There was a part of Emmy that held out hope that Aiden would pick up where he'd left off and kiss her again.

But there was another part of her that knew that wasn't a good idea.

So, without much conviction she said, "I should probably go."

"You probably should," he agreed with even less enthusiasm, kissing her again, though this time briefly and playfully.

And despite the fact that Emmy wanted to stay, to go on kissing him playfully and otherwise, that self-restraint she'd promised herself kicked in and told her she couldn't, that she had to leave before this went any further.

Still, she let herself have one more kiss. One that she instigated. One that lasted a little longer than those he'd been giving since the big one.

Then she took her hand from his face, pulled back and finally stood.

"This could get me into a lot of trouble," she told him.

"I won't tell if you won't," Aiden countered as he stood, too.

"You're my boss's friend. His fishing buddy."

"Your boss isn't here," Aiden said, running the backs of his fingers along her cheek in a light stroke that sent shivers down her spine and made her want to throw herself against him.

"And it's not as if I don't have anything at stake,"

he reminded, but in an almost whisper that was so quietly sexy it made her hot inside.

"All the more reason..." she said, her voice trailing off into a near purr in response to his touch, to everything he was doing to her just by being there.

"All the more reason," Aiden parroted with a resignation that said he understood. That he knew as well as she did that they shouldn't be doing what they were doing. What they'd done.

Then he kissed her again, anyway. Softly. Slowly. Sweetly. Before he said, "Go on. Go upstairs."

Emmy nodded her agreement but lifted her mouth to his for just one more kiss as a send off.

Then she forced herself to move. To go all the way out of the cabin without looking back.

But it didn't matter that she'd denied herself the parting glimpse of him that she craved. Even without it she knew that something had a grip on her when it came to Aiden Tarlington.

Something powerful.

Something that scoffed at the very notion of self-restraint and sent her up the stairs to the attic room quivering for more of what she'd just left behind.

So, so much more...

Chapter Six

"Emmy...Emmy..."

In her dream Emmy wasn't at all surprised that Aiden called her name. Why wouldn't he? They were lying on a picnic blanket in a meadow full of flowers with a warm summer sun shining brightly down on them.

"Emmy..."

His hands were in her hair, and hers were pressed to his amazing pectorals, and even though he was kissing her—long, slow, deep kisses—in between them he was saying her name as he nuzzled her neck and nibbled her earlobe....

"Emmy! Wake up!"

Wake up? What kind of an endearment was that? Then Emmy *did* wake up, with a jolt, as she realized Aiden wasn't only with her in her dreams. He was outside the attic's door, pounding on it and trying to rouse her in a completely unromantic way.

"Just a minute," she called back, struggling out of the fog, nearly lunging from her bed as if she'd been caught napping on the job.

She pulled on her bathrobe over the T-shirt and sweatpants she'd been sleeping in, shivering against the chill that had crept into the room since she'd turned off the space heater. Then she ran to unlock and open the door.

"I'm sorry to wake you," Aiden said, standing on the landing looking a little sleep-disheveled himself, despite the fact that he, at least, was dressed in a pair of jeans and a sweatshirt.

"What time is it?" she asked since it was still pitch-black outside.

"Not quite four o'clock. I have an emergency. Sounds like a heart attack. Can you come stay with Mickey while I get to this guy?"

"Sure." Emmy responded more to the urgency in his tone. The words took a bit longer to sink in.

"Put something on your feet and grab your coat," Aiden instructed when she didn't jump into action. "You can go back to sleep downstairs. But you have to hurry. I need to go."

Of course he did. Someone's life could depend on it, she realized somewhat sluggishly.

It finally put her into motion, however. Her slippers were beside the bed and once she'd jammed her feet into them she grabbed her coat, and followed Aiden out into the cold.

"I'll let you know what's going on when I can. Feel free to use my bed," he said as they reached his front door and he turned away from it to head for his SUV. "Thanks for this. I know it isn't what you came here to do," he added as he climbed into the vehicle.

Then he was gone, and Emmy was still standing on the porch, in a daze.

Surprisingly, it wasn't the chilly air that got through to her first, though. The sound of Aiden's car faded away within moments of him speeding off, and what penetrated Emmy's sleepy haze was the utter darkness beyond the inconsequential glow of the porch light. The stillness.

The fact that she was all alone out here.

And she didn't like it.

A second shiver shook her, but this one had nothing to do with the temperature, and she went inside in a rush, closing the door behind her and locking it as if something could test its strength at any moment.

Being in the warm, familiar cabin helped calm most of her sudden bout of uneasiness, and she decided the best remedy for the rest of it was to get back to sleep.

But before she could let herself do that, she thought she should check on Mickey to make sure he hadn't been disturbed by Aiden's emergency call. So she sloughed off her coat—dropping it on the overstuffed chair—and padded into Aiden's bedroom.

The baby's slumber was uninterrupted by what had

gone on. He was on his back in the crib, his little head turned to the side and his eyes closed.

His tiny hands were in gentle fists up around his face, and Emmy didn't think she'd ever seen anything quite as sweet as Mickey at that moment.

It made her want to scoop him into her arms, to cuddle up with him under a pile of heavy quilts and just hold him all night.

It made her want to have a baby of her own.

But that thought, that longing, was cut short when a loud clatter outside yanked her out of her reverie.

Her first thought was that Aiden had returned for some reason.

But why would he when any delay put his patient in more jeopardy?

So if it wasn't Aiden, who was it?

That sent a fresh wave of nervousness through her, and she was aware all over again that she was suddenly—and very much—on her own. In the middle of nowhere. With a helpless infant to keep safe.

Maybe the wind was blowing, she told herself. Maybe it had just blown something over.

That seemed possible. More likely, in fact, than that Aiden had come back or that there was anyone else outside.

Except that she hadn't noticed any wind when she'd come down the stairs from the attic or when she'd been on the porch only a few minutes earlier.

But it could have just started....

And since she wasn't hearing anything else, she hoped she could just forget about it.

She pulled Mickey's blanket up closer to his chin and smoothed the feathers of his hair, reveling in the downy softness.

But then another, louder crash came.

The wind. It's only the wind, she told herself.

But by then she didn't think she had any choice but to investigate.

So, with her heart halfway to her throat, she went to the back-facing window of Aiden's room to just barely peek through the side of the curtains that covered it.

She didn't hear any wind and there were clouds obscuring the moonglow, making it difficult to see much of anything outside.

Then she did see something. Or at least enough of something to make her catch her breath.

There was someone out there. Someone too shadowed to tell more than that he was big and hulking. Too big and hulking to be Aiden. And near the garbage cans.

Emmy froze.

Call 911, she told herself in a panic.

Then it occurred to her that maybe dialing 911 in the boondocks of Alaska didn't do what it did in populated areas. And even if it did put her in touch with a dispatcher who could send help, how long would it take for that help to actually arrive?

Too long when there was already a big hulk at the back door.

The back door.

Was it locked?

Nora Finley didn't lock her doors. Aiden didn't seem too conscientious about it, either.

Which meant that the back door could be unlocked. Easy entrance if the big hulk merely tried the knob.

She had to get to it. To check it. To lock it if it wasn't already.

Emmy let go of the curtains and ran like crazy out of Aiden's bedroom.

As she passed the light switch in the living room she swiped at it to turn off the light so whoever was outside wouldn't be able to see in. And when she reached the mud room and noticed the window in the top half of the back door, she dived to the floor so she wouldn't be seen there either, crawling the rest of the way.

The door *wasn't* locked and despite the fact that she managed to lock it before the intruder had found that out and gotten in, her heart was pounding so hard it made her light-headed.

What was she going to do? What if the intruder broke the lock? Or the window so he could just reach inside and let himself in, anyway?

She couldn't just sit idly by and let that happen. For Mickey's sake if not her own. She had to protect the baby no matter what she might be facing.

So she needed a weapon—that was the conclusion she came to. She needed something she could use to defend herself and Mickey with if she had to.

There was a broom hanging on the wall. There was a plunger under the washbasin. And there was a baseball bat propped in the corner.

Emmy crawled on all fours to snatch up the baseball bat as another loud bang came from just beyond the door.

This was one clumsy intruder, she thought.

Maybe he was drunk. Or hurt. Maybe it was someone who was hurt and looking for the doctor. Maybe his balance was so bad he was banging into things in his attempt to get to the door. Or maybe he *couldn't* get to the door and was signaling for help by hitting the trash cans.

She was going to have to take a second look.

But again, drawing attention to herself worried her, so she only inched upward—staying on her knees in front of the door—until her eyes alone cleared the wooden portion to peer through the lowest part of the glass.

In the time since she'd looked out the bedroom window, the clouds had moved away from the moon. Just enough to cast a small amount of light on the situation. Enough for her to see one of the trash cans overturned.

Enough to see that her intruder was neither human nor hurt.

It was a bear.

A very large brown bear.

For a moment Emmy relaxed. She breathed a sigh of relief. She even laughed at herself. At the unreasonable level of fear she'd felt.

Until it occurred to her that it wasn't as if she were in a zoo, where ferocious animals were contained and it was safe to pause and admire them. She was in the wild. She and Mickey. And they could very well be at the mercy of a deadly animal.

News reports of maulings flashed through her mind, and a whole new fear replaced the one she'd had of a man being outside.

And it didn't help that at that instant the bear stood on its hind legs, stretching to what must have been a full eight feet.

Emmy knew that one swipe of its enormous paw would be enough to take out the glass she was watching it through. And then what? How much use would a baseball bat be against an eight-foot bear?

Maybe she could scare it away before that happened, she thought as she again considered what to do. If she turned on the light outside would that be enough to frighten it into running off?

But what if the light frightened it but the bear didn't run off? Then she'd be confronting a scared, angry animal. A *huge,* scared, angry animal.

Not a good idea.

She knew she needed an equalizer. Something that would give her an advantage. Any advantage.

Pepper spray!

Wasn't that why she had that in her purse? So that if she were ever mugged she could use it to blind an attacker and get away? Maybe it would work the same way on a bear. And then at least she might be able to snatch Mickey out of his crib and run.

But her purse and the pepper spray were in the attic room.

Certainly she couldn't go upstairs to get them.

Even if she wanted to risk slipping out the front and climbing the stairs to the attic, there was no way she could leave Mickey down here.

So what could she use to replace pepper spray?

Hair spray? That would blind anything. But she doubted Aiden had hairspray.

What about something in the kitchen? Maybe he had something she could use there.

She didn't want the bear to catch sight of her any more than she'd wanted the imaginary intruder to, so she crawled from the mud room into the kitchen to search for any sort of weapon.

The only thing she found was a can of vegetable spray but even that seemed better than nothing, and she took it with her as she returned to the back door again.

Another crash from outside ripped through the silence of the night, and although Emmy had no idea what the bear had done to cause it, it didn't help calm her fears.

Armed with the baseball bat and the cooking spray, she hunkered down at the door, leaning all of her weight into it as if that would hold it fast against the enormous animal should it change its course.

But she was terrified that she didn't have anything at her disposal that would ultimately succeed against an enormous raging animal if it came to that.

"Just go away," she whispered. "Please, just go away."

And then she closed her eyes tight and prayed that bears were vegetarians, that this particular bear's appetite would be satisfied by something it dug out of the trash.

And that it wouldn't opt for making her its dinner and Mickey its dessert.

"Emmy?"

This time it didn't take more than a single utterance of her name for Emmy to wake with a start.

On the mud room floor next to the back door.

Baseball bat in one hand, cooking spray in the other, and both of them brought up instantly in defense.

"Wait! Wait! It's just me," Aiden said, taking a step back and out of harm's way.

Emmy came to her senses, going rapidly from reflex to realization and lowering her weapons.

She must have fallen asleep waiting for the bear to stop foraging and leave.

"Is Mickey all right?" she demanded.

"He must be, I can hear him chattering to himself in his crib," Aiden assured her.

Only when she knew the baby was safe did she give thought to the fact that Aiden was finally there, standing above her where she sat on the floor against the door, ready to attack anything that moved with a baseball bat and cooking spray. And that the sun was up and the bear was gone....

"What's going on?" Aiden asked as she got to her feet on joints that were stiff from the awkward position she'd been in for hours.

"A bear," she said with all the weightiness she

thought that information carried. "Just after you left I heard noises in the backyard. At first I thought it was you and then I thought it was a burglar. But it was a bear. A huge brown bear."

Aiden's expression wasn't what she expected in reaction to the news. There was no shock. No alarm. But there was sympathy.

"That must have really scared you," he said with a small smile. "Are you going to hit me if I give you a hug?"

"No," she said without thinking about it, too weary and worn-out to fight against something that sounded like the perfect antidote to her frazzled nerves.

And it was, too. Aiden stepped forward and wrapped his long, muscular arms around her, engulfing her in the warmth and power of a body that seemed invincible.

Emmy let herself truly relax for the first time since he'd left. She rested her cheek against his chest where she could hear the steady beat of his heart. Where the heat and power of him could seep into her and make everything seem all right again. Even if she was still clinging to the baseball bat and the cooking spray.

Then, gently, compassionately, but with some amusement in his tone, Aiden said, "So did you think sitting against the door would stop the bear from coming into the house?"

Being in his arms felt so good, so reassuring, that she was beginning to feel more like herself again. It kept her from taking offense at the edge of humor in his voice and allowed her to merely explain her panicked thinking. "I was sitting against the door so the bear wouldn't see me and I could fight it off before it got to Mickey if it did get in."

"Okay. So you were going to fight a bear with a baseball bat. And what were you going to do with the cooking stuff? Make it slippery enough to slide it right into the frying pan for breakfast?"

It did seem a little silly now and even Emmy managed to smile slightly at the idea. "I thought I could spray the bear in the face and blind it to give myself more of a chance to hit it and then get to Mickey."

"Okay," he repeated. Then he lost his composure and laughed but only lightly before he apologized for it.

"I'm sorry. I know a bear in the backyard is a big deal to you and you really were probably frightened half to death."

"Does that mean you would have thought it was nothing at all?" she asked, lifting her head away from his chest so she could look up at him.

Aiden released his hold enough to accommodate it but he didn't let go of her completely. "It's just something that happens around here. In fact, one of the favorite things to do on a first date is to park by the local dump and watch the bears digging through the refuse."

"Are you trying to tell me that I was terrified by what's ordinarily first-date entertainment?"

His smile stretched into a grin that confirmed that. "We keep the lids closed tight on the trash cans around our houses in hopes that they won't attract the bears. But sometimes the bears come anyway—especially in the spring when they're just out of hibernation and they're hungry, and in the fall when they're packing on weight for the winter's sleep. They can do some damage but I've never known one yet to bother with breaking and entering. Not that you could know that,'' he was quick to add. ''How big was he?''

''At least ten feet tall,'' she exaggerated for effect.

''And did Mickey sleep through it all?''

''He did. But now you have me thinking I should have gotten him up to watch the show.''

''I didn't say that.'' But his expression said he'd thought it. ''And you ended up sleeping on the floor to guard the door for him. That's pretty good.''

''It didn't feel good,'' Emmy said, rolling her aching shoulders for emphasis.

But that did more than she'd intended it to. It pushed her breasts into his chest in a way that seemed to accentuate how little separated her bare breasts from his naked chest—nothing more than her thin T-shirt and his simple sweatshirt. Not enough to hide the fact that the contact had hardened her nipples instantly.

Emmy knew Aiden had felt it. How could he not have?

For a moment they stood there in a state of limbo as he looked down into her eyes and she peered up into his. And the question of where to go from there seemed to linger in the air.

Emmy stopped thinking about bears and instead focused on Aiden and the kiss they'd shared the night before. And on how much she would like it if he'd kiss her again now. And on him answering the unintentional invitation of her insistent nipples by slipping his hands under her T-shirt. And so many things that had nothing at all to do with the hours and the fear that had just passed.

But then Aiden turned Emmy so that her back was to him and he began massaging her shoulders like a boxer's trainer before a big fight, putting an end to the moment.

It was the wiser choice, Emmy told herself.

But it was still a bit of a letdown.

Then she aided the cause by introducing a safer subject, too.

"How is your patient?" she asked.

There was another moment during which she thought Aiden was reconsidering their altered course. But then he seemed to concede to it, too, and answered her as he continued to rub her shoulders.

"I have him stabilized for the time being, but I've called the hospital in Fairbanks to send their helicopter for him. He needs to spend a few days being observed and having some tests done to see where we stand and what we need to do to prevent another attack."

"It was his heart, then?"

"No doubt about it."

"Where is he now?"

"The only place I have to put him—on a cot in my

office with Maria keeping an eye on him so I could sneak back here for a shower.''

A shower sounded good. Together…

''And a shave,'' she added with a glance back at him and the thick growth of whiskers that gave him more sexy, scruffy, mountain-man appeal than she could endure.

Then another quarter was heard from as Mickey let it be known he was bored with entertaining himself in the other room and needed someone to pay some attention to him.

''Looks like getting me cleaned up will have to wait, though,'' Aiden said. ''I'll have to take care of our boy before I can do anything else.''

Emmy had no idea why—maybe it was the fact that she'd just spent the past several hours feeling as protective of the baby as she would have felt if he were her own—but today she wanted to be the one to go in and get Mickey up, to hold him the way she'd wanted to during the night, to reassure herself he was all right.

''I'll change him and feed him while you shower,'' she heard herself say then. ''When you're finished you can give him his bath while I go upstairs to dress.''

That surprised Aiden. ''You will? That'd be great. Then we can get back into the office sooner.''

His massage stopped suddenly and he leaned over one of those shoulders he'd been ministering to. ''You're not offering just to postpone going outside, are you? Because I just came in and there aren't any bears to be seen. Although you are still armed.''

Emmy had gotten so used to hanging on to the bat and the spray she'd forgotten she still had them.

''Very funny,'' she said in answer to his question.

But he wasn't finished teasing her yet because as Emmy stepped out of his grasp to return the baseball bat to the corner and then faced Aiden again he was grinning broadly. ''You were awfully cute huddled against that door, though,'' he said.

''I wasn't *huddled*,'' Emmy said, taking issue with his terminology.

''Okay. But you were cute all the same.''

''Oh, right,'' Emmy muttered facetiously, thinking how not cute she must really look in her inelegant pajamas, without makeup and her hair a mess.

Then Mickey sent up a loud wail and cut short their banter.

Emmy tossed Aiden the vegetable spray like an expert pitcher and said, ''Hit the showers, wise guy.''

She bypassed him with a strut to her walk that completely belied the throes of terror she'd been in only a short time earlier.

The day was another hectic one at Aiden's office—made more so by the need to keep a close eye on his heart attack patient. Plus, in the middle of everything, Aiden had to deal with transporting the man to the hospital helicopter that finally arrived to pick him up.

Emmy spent the hours doing what she'd done every other day—following Aiden around to observe and make notes. The only difference was in the new emotions she found herself experiencing over Mickey. Emotions that left her feeling protective of him and somewhat proprietary. Feelings that gave her a greater understanding of what her predecessor had had problems with.

It wasn't easy, she realized, to move into a community like Boonesbury, to be made a part of the everyday living and not get involved.

But like her attraction to Aiden, she warned herself to keep Mickey in perspective, too.

Because in a few days she'd be leaving them both behind.

And that was something she couldn't lose sight of.

When the day finally ended Aiden suggested that— if Emmy wasn't too tired—they have dinner at the Boonesbury Inn and stay in town for the big bonfire that kicked off the high school homecoming festivities.

Emmy agreed. She was beginning to suffer the effects of her night of limited sleep, but the event sounded interesting and, despite not much rest himself, Aiden seemed to want to go.

The event had brought more people than usual into town so the inn was bustling. Rather than wait for a table of their own, Aiden, Emmy and Mickey accepted an invitation to share one with the local barber and his wife—Herman and Sonia Morse.

The couple was more interested in Mickey than anything. The barber wanted Aiden to know that he'd asked every one of his clients since hearing about Mickey if they knew who the baby might belong to, but hadn't garnered any information, either. And Sonia—who was Boonesbury's sole postal clerk— had also mounted a campaign by questioning her customers, and reported that she, too, had learned nothing.

Their tenacity struck Emmy as odd until they began to ask what would happen to the baby in the long run and made it clear that they would be interested in adopting him, that after ten years of infertility tests and treatments, they'd decided other methods of starting a family needed to be considered.

Aiden was better with that than Emmy. He assured the couple that he'd keep them in mind. But although Emmy said very little, she found herself lifting the baby out of his carrier to hold him on her lap as if the barber and his wife might snatch Mickey away at any moment.

And no amount of reminding herself to keep things in perspective could make her loosen her possessive hold on the child.

After the meal, Emmy and Aiden retrieved Aiden's SUV to drive to the outskirts of town where a huge pyramid of timber and twigs was already waiting.

A surprisingly large crowd gathered in support of the school as the fire was lit and a display of Native American folk dance began around it.

Emmy watched in fascination as things she'd only seen on television or in movies were performed right there in front of her.

First, five Inuit men danced. Garbed in ankle-length red robes with hoods that framed their faces in white fur, they answered the call of a plaintive song with a vigorous, primitive parade around the perimeters of the flames.

Then a Native American woman wearing a ceremonial dress and feathers in her hair, did a straightbacked, dignified step, following the same path as female voices chanted an accompaniment that kept time with the steady pounding of the drums that provided rhythm. Drums that infected the celebration with excitement, building in anticipation, in intensity, until they came to an abrupt stop.

The sudden silence was deafening, and for a moment it almost seemed to Emmy as if her heart had stopped beating, too. Until everyone broke into applause and cheers and whistles of appreciation.

Boonesbury's mayor stepped up to a microphone to announce who would be this year's homecoming queen and king. The two teenagers called to the podium to be crowned were greeted with more enthusiastic whistling and clapping.

Then the school band—which was actually a quintet—played the school song to usher in the two boys and one girl who would be representing the school in the homecoming archery tournament that replaced the football game that marked the beginning of the year in schools big enough to have a team.

Another loud beating of the drums and more applause welcomed them as if they were local heroes and then quieted so they could prove their prowess by simultaneously firing flaming arrows into the ground in exactly the same spot.

When the cheers had died down, the mayor invited everyone to the dance the next night, encouraging attendance to fill in the ranks of the handful of kids old enough to go themselves.

"Is this where they bring out the marshmallows for toasting?" Emmy asked when the formal entertainments ended and everyone just began milling around or continuing to watch the fire still blazing brightly in the center of it all.

Aiden bent close to her ear and said, "Shh... This is a sacred fire. Marshmallows would be sacrilegious."

"Oops."

"But we could go home and get out of the cold and have a fire of our own. Toast marshmallows there," he suggested.

Emmy wasn't sure if it only seemed intimate and slightly seductive because he was still speaking directly into her ear, his breath warm against her skin, or if he was infusing the offer with that intimacy and seductiveness on purpose.

But either way, making the whole fire thing a private affair in Aiden's heated cabin was too appealing an idea for Emmy to refuse.

"You have marshmallows?" she asked, hearing a tinge of intimacy in her own tone.

"I do, actually."

She wasn't sure she believed him, but it didn't matter. It wasn't the marshmallows she was really interested in, anyway.

"Okay, then. Let's go."

"Great," Aiden said as though surprised—and pleased—that she'd agreed.

Then he placed a sure hand at the small of her back to guide her to the truck again, carrying the car seat in his other hand.

Mickey, who had been enthralled by the spectacle of the bonfire, fell asleep on the ride home.

Emmy offered to get him to bed while Aiden went upstairs to turn on her space heater and then build their private fire in the stone fireplace in his living room.

By the time Emmy had tucked Mickey in—and had given him a secret kiss good-night—Aiden had a roaring blaze going, a blanket spread out in front of it and couch cushions upturned against the coffee table to brace their backs so they'd be comfortable.

"Marshmallows and a skewer," Aiden said from the kitchen behind her as Emmy took in the scene.

"You really do have marshmallows," she said with a laugh, glancing over her shoulder at him.

"You doubted me?" he said as if he were injured. Then he cracked a smile to let her know he was kidding. "I had a Fourth of July barbecue and somebody brought them and left them."

"Two-month-old marshmallows?" Emmy made a face.

"Is that a bad thing?"

"They might be a little stale."

"Marshmallows get stale?" he repeated as if it were unfathomable to him.

"Everything gets stale," Emmy informed.

"Not everything," Aiden said pointedly, making her think he was talking about her company and not about food anymore. At least not until he added, "I guess we'll just have to try 'em and see."

Aiden came into the living room and motioned Emmy to the fireplace ahead of him.

She obliged, and as she situated herself on one portion of the blanket she watched him as he came to stand at the very edge of it.

He didn't look any the worse for wear after a long night and an even longer day fueled by a scant few hours of sleep. He had on a pair of khaki-colored twill jeans and a hunter-green sweater-knit long-sleeved polo shirt, and he'd shaved at some point after they'd gotten home so he smelled wonderfully of that woodsy scent he used for aftershave.

Emmy just hoped she looked as good. She was confident her gray slacks and matching V-neck T-shirt had held up, but wished she'd been able to put a brush through her hair since she'd taken it out of the band and combed it to fall free around her shoulders just before they'd left the office.

But then Aiden joined her on the blanket and she was struck by how wonderful it was just to be alone with him, to have him all to herself, and she forgot to worry about her appearance.

He opened the bag of marshmallows and jabbed

two of them on the single skewer. In order to hold them close enough to the fire to toast them he had to sit nearer the flames than Emmy was. He did that, facing the hearth and leaving her with a view of his broad back.

She didn't mind. Except that just looking at his wide shoulders and the narrowing vee down to his waist gave her a sudden urge to lay both her hands flat against that muscular expanse. An urge so intense it was difficult to fight.

But conversation seemed like the best remedy, and so she said the first thing that came to mind.

"I was surprised by the barber's and his wife's open campaign for Mickey."

"Herman and Sonia?"

"Mmm."

Aiden must have been able to tell by her tone that the couple had rubbed her wrong because he said, "Don't be too hard on them. They've gone through a lot to have a baby and nothing has worked. It's actually good that they've moved forward to thinking about adoption."

"But what if Mickey is *your* baby?" Emmy said, hearing a defensiveness she hadn't meant to put in her tone.

"Then Herman and Sonia wanting him is a moot point," Aiden answered reasonably.

Emmy was beginning to wonder how he could be so patient about being left in the dark over something that could alter his whole life. "Do you think it's possible you'll never hear from Nora Finley?'' she asked.

Apparently Aiden was realizing how antsy she felt regarding this subject, though, because he said, "I'm not worried about Nora contacting me. You just can't expect too much too soon. There's no hurry here, and you have to keep that in mind."

"But what if she doesn't come back or contact you at all?" Emmy insisted.

The marshmallows were golden brown and Aiden pulled the skewer away from the heat so they could share them. "If Nora never shows up or calls me or gets a message to me—and no one else comes to claim Mickey either—then I'll do a DNA test to determine if he is or isn't mine," Aiden said, clearly having thought about this eventuality.

"And if he is yours?"

"Then he is. I'll raise him."

"By yourself?"

Aiden gave her an amused little smile and glanced around the cabin. "By myself, yes. Unless you see somebody coming out of the woodwork that I don't."

"But what about times like last night, when you don't have anyone else here?"

"If you hadn't been here I would have taken him with me. Granted it wouldn't have been as convenient for me or to Mickey's advantage, but it would have worked out."

"And if he *isn't* yours? What then? Have you thought about keeping him anyway?"

Aiden didn't answer that readily. But when he did,

it seemed honest—even if it wasn't exactly what Emmy wanted to hear.

"If Mickey isn't mine, well, people like Herman and Sonia would make great parents and he deserves that—a full set. Hard as it would be for me to give him up," Aiden finished in a way that let Emmy know he didn't like the idea any more than she did.

He was toasting two more of the fluffy white pillows of sugar but he spared her a look over his shoulder then. "Am I mistaken or have you gotten a little attached to our boy Mickey?"

Okay, so maybe it had been obvious today.

But all Emmy would admit to was, "He's a cute baby."

Aiden once again let her have the first marshmallow on the skewer, taking the second for himself as he said, "Have you not wanted to have kids of your own up to now? Or have you just not gotten around to it? Or not had the chance?"

He seemed to be changing the subject. Maybe because it was painful for him to think about giving Mickey up. It was painful for Emmy, although she didn't want to consider why that might be. So she rolled with the altered topic and answered his question.

"I had the chance. Well, technically," she said to qualify it. "I was married for over five years. If the marriage had lasted, the plan was to get pregnant about now—at twenty-nine—so the first baby would be born when we were thirty."

"Sounds like a wise idea," Aiden said as he went

on to round three of the marshmallows. "But here you are—single and not on the verge of starting a family. What happened?"

She hadn't wanted to talk about this with Aiden before. In fact, she'd only alluded to it when she'd told him about her career path and she'd sidestepped the subject the previous evening.

But now it didn't seem like such a big deal to be open with him, to share her past a little.

"I was married to Jon Charles Claiborne, attorney-at-law," she said with a laugh at her own grandiosity. "At least he was an attorney-at-law when I met him and for the first three years of our marriage."

"Then what was he?"

"Then he was a grape-grower-vintner-wannabe."

"Huh?"

Emmy smiled. "I know, it's quite a leap," she said with more of an edge of venom than she'd intended.

"Explain, please," Aiden requested.

Emmy curbed her animosity. "Jon was an ambitious lawyer one day, and—literally the next day—he came home, told me he'd quit his job and bought a vineyard. That I should pack my bags, call Howard to tell him I'd never be in again and load up the car because we were going to grow grapes and make wine."

Aiden offered her the latest gooey treat and, as Emmy took it, she let him know it was her last.

He polished off the final marshmallow, set the skewer on the hearth and eased himself to sit beside her with his back on the couch cushion and one arm stretched out behind her so he could sit angled toward her.

Then, when he was comfortable, he said, "And were you *willing* to pack up, resign, grow grapes and make wine?"

"No, I wasn't, as a matter of fact. But thanks for asking—it's more than my husband bothered to do."

"But willing or not, you went along anyway?"

"My choices were do it or end my marriage on the spot, because Jon was going with or without me."

"Nice," Aiden said facetiously.

"Yeah, not very."

"So you went?"

"I went," Emmy confirmed.

"To the heart of the beautiful Napa Valley?" Aiden asked, as if that might redeem the other man.

"Oh, no. To a little backwater not much bigger— or fancier—than Boonesbury."

"And you had to leave the foundation—that was that hiatus you mentioned before, wasn't it?"

"Yes, that was when I was on hiatus from the foundation," Emmy said. "I had to be. A total lifestyle change was what Jon set out to accomplish, and that's what we got. He'd invested everything we had in the place, and we couldn't afford help with the vineyard, so farmhand had to become my job."

"You didn't go into it loving the idea, and I'm assuming you didn't grow to love it, either," Aiden said.

"No. I didn't like being away from everything— friends, my work, conveniences. I also didn't like the *lifestyle* Jon adopted for us. He was happy as a lark playing Farmer Brown but I wasn't. Not that I'm saying there's anything wrong with it if that's what a person chooses, but it isn't what I chose or what I was cut out for or what I enjoyed doing. Although, to be honest, it's hard to enjoy anything when you're so full of resentment.''

''You resented the work?''

''The work was actually at the bottom of the list. More, I resented that I hadn't had a say in the big move. I resented the ultimatum he'd given me to get me there. I resented him.'' Emmy paused a moment to get past the catch in her throat that this subject could still cause.

Then she said, ''It was the resentment that really ended up destroying the marriage. So, by a year and a half after we'd made the *big move,* I was back in L.A., starting over again at the foundation and filing for divorce,'' she finished with the full impact of that decision echoing in her voice.

Aiden's expression was understanding and sympathetic. ''It's amazingly tough, isn't it?'' he commented as he ran the backside of his index finger along her cheek, soothing away some of her stress. ''I mean, there's so much divorce now it almost seems like it must be easy. But when it's *your* divorce, it's not easy at all.''

''No, it isn't,'' Emmy agreed.

It was, however, easy to fall under the spell of him caressing her face and the heat of those deep-set, sparkling blue eyes as they peered down into hers. A spell that might have begun with the intent of comforting but had become something else entirely. Something that set aside the hurts of the past and reminded Emmy that in spite of them she was still alive and thriving and very much aware of the fact that she was sitting here with the most incredibly handsome, masculine, sexy man she'd ever met.

The man she was so attracted to it was as if that attraction had a life of its own. A will of its own.

The man who had kissed her into oblivion last night.

Suddenly all that they had just talked about seemed distant and far away. Everything but the two of them seemed unimportant. And all Emmy really wanted was to have Aiden kiss her again the way he'd kissed her before....

Maybe looking so deeply into her eyes allowed him to read her mind because that finger that was stroking her face moved to just beneath her chin to tip her face up to his.

Then he did exactly what she'd been unwittingly willing him to do—he leaned forward just enough to press his mouth to hers.

And Emmy was lost. That quickly. With nothing more than one caress of her face, one touch of his parted lips to hers. All thought fled and she was caught up in the soft, sensual cocoon that wrapped around her as surely as his arms did, pulling her closer to him, deeper into the kiss.

His tongue came to tease the scant inner edge of

her lips, the tips of her teeth, before it found her tongue and gracefully enticed it.

Emmy was only too happy to comply, to meet him and dance, tongue to tongue, in a sweetly choreographed minuet as passion began all over again.

She reached her hands to Aiden's neck, feeling the strength there, testing the soft bristles of his hair where it curved at his nape before she let her hands do some traveling down that back she'd been so enthralled by moments earlier.

Broad and hard muscled, it felt as good as it looked. At least as good as it looked through his clothes.

But now that she had answered that urge to lay her hands there, she developed a new one. An urge to know how his back looked and felt without the shirt.

She was bone weary from her lack of sleep the previous night and maybe that relaxed some inhibitions because almost as soon as the fresh urge struck, Emmy responded to it, too. She tugged Aiden's shirt from the waistband of his pants and slid her hands underneath, up to his bare back.

Warm, smooth, silk-over-steel. Emmy reveled in it, gliding along the hills and valleys of honed muscles and taut tendons, drinking in the power contained there. The luxurious masculinity that was Aiden.

It spoke to the most feminine recesses of her, turning her nipples into tight pebbles that yearned for some attention of their own.

Somehow they had slipped down on the blanket, and Aiden eased her the rest of the way until Emmy was lying on her back and he was beside her, above her, still kissing her, only even deeper now as passion seemed to have gained a stronghold and grown more powerful, more demanding.

He was braced on one elbow, but his free hand was on her neck, doing some of that gentle massaging he was so good at.

There was nothing shy about him as his hand began a slow trace of the V-neckline of her sweater.

Every inch that he touched of her own bare skin awakened nerve endings, escalating her need for more.

Instead she got less. For a split second, anyway, as he abandoned her mouth to place tantalizing kisses to the underside of her chin, to the hollow of her throat where he flicked his tongue against her skin and left that spot to air dry when he went farther still to nuzzle his way under her sweater so he could kiss her collarbone.

But Emmy wanted—needed—much more than that.

So much more than that.

On their own, her head and shoulders drew back, her spine arched, and her hands moved forward, first to the bulge of his triceps, and then to his pectorals, demonstrating even as she explored.

Aiden raised upward again, taking her mouth with his again in a wide-open, plundering kiss that at first seemed to ignore the other message she was conveying.

But only for a moment before his hand slipped to

the side of her waist. Rubbing, caressing her there for a time before he found the hem of her sweater and made his way underneath it.

Big and hot and powerful, his hand was on her stomach. He played there, increasing her anticipation, her desire.

Then he rose to her rib cage. Kneading it, massaging again, titillating her with just a thumb that reached to only the lower curve of her breast to drive her nearly insane.

Until finally his whole hand reached her breast, taking it into his ample palm where her nipple greeted him with a tightened knot.

Her bra was nothing but a hint of lace, and yet Emmy regretted having worn it at all. It was just in the way, diluting the sensations she craved so much she thought she might burst.

But this time Aiden didn't torture her with delays, he found his way underneath the wisp of lace to grant her her heart's desire and engulf that engorged orb in the wonders of his touch.

And wondrous it was.

He seemed to know exactly what she needed. When she needed tenderness. When she needed not-so-tenderness. When to tease and torment. When to tug. When to brush whisper-light fingertips just across the tip and when to take her fully into his kneading hand.

And all this while his mouth kept hers engaged. While kisses heightened every pleasure, and the desire for even more started to climb.

The desire to have his mouth where only his hands had been till then.

The desire to have his hands on other parts of her body. Even more intimate parts.

The desire to have their naked bodies pressed together, entwined, united...

But even as those desires grew, so did Emmy's doubts, seeded in the memory of the pain that had come from that other relationship she'd just told him about.

"We should stop," she said in a weak, ragged voice full of reluctance once she'd forced herself to end their kiss.

"We should?" Aiden asked, his tone seductive, his hand at her breast working wonders, making her question her resolve all over again.

But now that the thoughts had begun she couldn't turn them off.

"We should," she confirmed. "I don't want to. But we should."

"If you don't want to..." He kissed her again, short, sexy little kisses.

"We still should," she insisted.

He didn't though. Not immediately. Instead he kissed her again—openmouthed, his tongue thrusting inside just the way she wanted other portions of him thrusting into other portions of her—and he clasped her breast ever more firmly even as he flicked his thumb against the crest to drive her crazier than he had before.

And *then* he stopped.

Kissing her.

Working his wonders at her breast.

And even though Emmy knew it was for the best, that it was what she'd told him to do, deep down she wanted to say, Never mind. Forget what I said. Just make love to me....

But she didn't.

Aiden sat up and helped her to sit up, too, watching her as he did.

"I'm not apologizing," he warned her. "It all felt too right."

It did to her, too.

"I know. But—"

"But what *wasn't* right was the time," he guessed.

The time. The place...

But rather than say that, she just agreed with his assumption and then said, "I just think I'd better go upstairs before we get too...carried away."

Aiden nodded, if not his agreement with that then at least his concession to it.

He stood and so did Emmy, straightening her clothes along the way.

"Another day at the office tomorrow?" she asked as he walked her to the door.

"At the office in the morning and teaching the birth prep class I had to cancel for today in the afternoon. Then tomorrow night is the homecoming dance. Would you be my date?" he asked like a teenage boy, except that his voice was already deep and rich— made more so by what they'd almost done.

"Tomorrow night will be my last night here,"

Emmy pointed out for no other reason except that it had just occurred to her.

"Then you'll be off the clock completely."

"Mmm," Emmy said, thinking that that might be a dangerous way to think about it.

"So that means this is just Emmy Harris being asked on a nonwork-related date by Aiden Tarlington. What do you say?"

"I say yes," she answered without having to think about it because the prospect was too appealing to deny herself.

Aiden smiled down at her. Pleased. "Good."

Then he kissed her again. Softly but with enough oomph to curl her toes all over again before he opened the door for her.

Emmy was tempted not to go through it. To stay and lose herself all over again in those kisses that had set this whole thing into motion.

But she fought the inclination and went outside.

"Good night," she said over her shoulder as she did.

"Yes, it was," Aiden responded.

And it was, too. Emmy couldn't refute that so she didn't try.

She just went upstairs to her cozy little attic room.

Trying hard not to think about how much cozier it would have been if Aiden had come up there with her....

Chapter Seven

Aiden was packing Mickey's makeshift diaper bag the next morning when his phone rang. He answered it, and from the other end of the line he heard, "Do I need to give you guys a refresher course on safe sex or what?"

Aiden laughed. "Hey, Dev," he said, recognizing his younger brother's voice. "Talked to Ethan, did you?"

"First him with the surprise baby bit and now you, too? What the hell's going on?"

"Good question."

"Ethan told me about this whole baby-on-the-doorstep deal," Devon said then. "Do we know yet if it's yours?"

"*It* is a he—Mickey—and no, we don't know yet

whether or not he's mine. I'm still waiting to hear from the woman who could be his mother.''

''But she's not rushing to talk to you?'' Devon said ominously.

''I don't know if that's the case or if she's just incommunicado for the time being. I'll give her a little longer before I start to read anything into it,'' Aiden said.

''Man, I can't believe this,'' Devon sighed. ''I called down to Ethan to have him check on things around my place, and when he said you might be a dad, too, I thought he was putting me on.''

''Nope.''

''So how are you doing with this?''

''I'm plugging along. There isn't much else I can do.''

''And is all this going on with the lady judge and jury there?''

Aiden knew his brother was referring to Emmy. ''The 'lady judge and jury's' name is Emmy Harris. And yes, this has all been going on with her here. It's been kind of strange, to say the least.''

''Guess you could have used me hanging around after all, then. To baby-sit, huh?''

Aiden laughed at the notion. Devon was about as far as anyone could be from domesticity. He wouldn't have known the first thing about what to do with a baby.

''We're doing okay,'' Aiden assured him.

''Is lady J and J still there?''

''She is.''

"And how *okay* are you doing with her?"

Aiden could tell by his brother's innuendo-laden tone that Ethan had spilled the beans about Aiden's attraction to Emmy, too. But he purposely misunderstood the intent of the question. "I think she's seeing for herself that Boonesbury needs and deserves the grant," he said instead.

"Is she seeing what you need and deserve and taking care of that, too?"

"Geez, Devon," Aiden groaned, not wanting to talk about Emmy that way, even though his younger sibling hadn't really said anything derogatory.

"Oh-oh, you're pretty touchy about her. You must like her," Devon teased.

"She's great," Aiden confirmed as if it were no big deal, even as the previous evening flashed through his mind and reminded him of just how big a deal Emmy was becoming to him.

"Then maybe, on second thought, it's a good thing I made myself scarce so you could be on your own with her," Devon said, changing his tune.

But Aiden thought that maybe it wasn't a good thing that he'd been on his own with Emmy. That maybe if Devon had stuck around, things would have stayed in some kind of safety zone. As it was they seemed to be venturing farther and farther onto thin ice.

But rather than getting into that with his brother, Aiden decided to change the subject. "Are you coming back here before you go home to Denver again?"

"Why? Don't you want me to?" Devon said, once

more making the conversation about Emmy and goading Aiden with insinuation.

"Of course I want you to. I barely got to say hello to you before you left again. And, as I recall, you originally came up here to take pictures and didn't."

"And if I come back will I get to meet the woman in question?"

"Only if you make it back before noon tomorrow. That's when she's scheduled to leave."

"Tomorrow? So soon?"

It did seem soon. Too soon. And it had been eating at Aiden since Emmy had announced that tonight would be her last night here.

"A? Are you there?"

Aiden had been lost in that thought for so long his brother must have wondered if the call had been cut off.

"Yeah, I'm still here."

"And your scrutinizer is really leaving town?" Devon reiterated.

"Afraid so," Aiden confirmed.

"Too bad."

"Too bad is right," Aiden muttered to himself. Then, not wanting to show too much of his reaction to his brother, he changed the subject. "Am I not enough of a draw to get you back to Boonesbury?"

"I suppose I better come back. Sounds to me like you'll probably need a shoulder to cry on once this Emmy Harris is gone," Devon said, sensing the change in Aiden's attitude since they'd been talking about Emmy's departure.

"Uh-huh," was Aiden's only comment—a verbal rolling of the eyes.

"I'll be in on Sunday," Devon said. "Think you can get by that long without me?"

"I can never be sure, but I'll do my damnedest," Aiden retorted sarcastically.

"Look for me then, then."

"You know to just come in and make yourself at home if I'm out on an emergency or something, right?"

"You mean you're still practicing medicine in the middle of this soap opera?" Devon joked.

"A little here and there."

"What do you do with the kid when you're working?"

"Take him along."

"Weird."

"Less than you might think," Aiden answered, realizing for the first time how easily he'd slipped into the whole parenthood thing—the whole family thing, really, with Emmy in the picture—and how much he'd actually enjoyed it....

"Guess I'll see you Sunday," Devon said, interrupting Aiden's wandering thoughts.

"Good," Aiden countered.

"Hope you hear from Mickey's mother in the meantime and you're off the hook as a dad."

"Mmm," was all Aiden said in response before they exchanged goodbyes and hung up.

But even after he had, he still wasn't sure whether

he hoped he was off the hook as Mickey's dad or not. Not anymore.

Because that phone call from his younger brother had caused him to think about Mickey and Emmy in a whole different light.

And suddenly he couldn't honestly say he would be happy to lose either of them.

Emmy never traveled without packing an all-purpose, just-in-case black dress. So that morning, after she'd had her bath, she took the dress out of her suitcase and hung it in the steamy bathroom to relax the wrinkles.

The dress was a simple, midcalf-length wrap with three-quarter sleeves, and as she smoothed it, Emmy felt silly admitting even to herself how much she was looking forward to the homecoming dance. In fact, she was looking forward to it as much as she'd looked forward to her own school dances long ago.

Of course, if she were honest with herself, she had to admit that it was probably not the dance alone that had her anticipation level so high.

It was more likely the opportunity to be with Aiden. On a real date. On a real date she was planning to dress up for.

She wondered what he would wear. If he'd wear a suit. Or maybe only a sport coat. If whatever he wore would have been bought at the general store where he'd taken her to buy her coat and warmer clothes.

But even as she considered the worst of the possibilities—that he would wear something he'd just bought off the general store's rack and that it would be saggy and baggy—she still couldn't picture him not being attractive.

But then how could she when she'd never seen him look *un*attractive regardless of what he had on? No, no matter what he wore, he'd still be drop-dead gorgeous. More drop-dead gorgeous than anyone she'd ever gone to a school dance with, that was for sure.

But she couldn't deny that it would be nice if that drop-dead gorgeousness was cloaked in something special. If just once before she left she got to see him all decked out....

Something about that thought jabbed at Emmy and it took her a moment to pinpoint what it was.

And then it came to her.

Just once before she *left...*

This would be her last night in Boonesbury. In Alaska. Her last night with Aiden.

And as if she hadn't known it before, when it struck her, it sort of knocked the wind out of her.

She was leaving tomorrow. *Tomorrow.* She was going back to L.A.

While Aiden stayed in Boonesbury.

It wasn't as if she hadn't known it all along. She just hadn't thought about it. Until now. Now, when it had sneaked up on her. Like the end of a vacation.

A vacation? Was she really comparing this trip—a business trip—to a vacation? This trip that had begun so badly she'd suspected it was a setup to test her stamina? How could this be on a level with a cruise to the Bahamas or a tour of Europe?

But this last week had actually been better than the cruise she'd taken to the Bahamas and the tour of Europe put together.

And there was only one reason for it. Aiden.

Aiden who she would be leaving behind.

Aiden and Mickey...

Emmy suddenly deflated, sitting on the edge of the claw-footed bathtub, no longer looking forward to Boonesbury's homecoming dance.

How could she when being at that dance tonight would mean she was that much closer to the time she'd have to say goodbye to Aiden—goodbye to Mickey—forever?

No, she definitely hadn't been thinking about this trip ending.

Not that she'd made a conscious choice not to think about it. But maybe it had been an unconscious one. An unconscious choice to protect herself from just what she felt as the reality sank in—heartsick.

Was this what Evelyn had done on those other trips? she wondered. Was this being too involved in other-than-grant affairs? Was this the kind of thing that had clouded her predecessor's judgment and caused her such emotional turmoil that she hadn't done her job well and had lost all perspective?

Emmy was convinced that in Evelyn's same position she *had* done all it was her duty to do. And that she hadn't lost her perspective. At least not where the grant and the foundation were concerned.

But the emotional turmoil?

She had plenty of that.

She certainly couldn't deny that she was involved with Aiden and with Mickey, too. That they'd somehow gotten under her skin.

And although she didn't believe it was clouding her judgment, she was also feeling more a wreck with every passing moment.

So what was she going to do about it? she asked herself.

But she didn't have an answer.

And no matter how hard she tried, she couldn't come up with one. What she felt, she felt, and she couldn't just cancel it out.

But what she felt wasn't going to make it easy when the time came to leave them.

When the time came to leave them *tomorrow*....

But tomorrow wasn't here yet, she reminded herself. She still had today. And tonight.

And if she was going to accept that this trip had turned out to seem like a vacation, then she should treat these last precious hours the way she would treat the last precious hours of a vacation, too. Which meant that she couldn't think about tomorrow at all.

''Think about the next few minutes, the next hour. Not the end,'' she advised herself.

That was how she kept the finish of a vacation from being ruined. She didn't think about the vacation coming to an end until she was repacking to go and it really was over.

And that was what she had to do now, she knew.

Because if she didn't, those final hours she had would be ruined. And she didn't want that. She wanted to be able to enjoy them, to enjoy Aiden, to enjoy every minute she had left with him. Every minute she had left with Mickey.

That was what she was determined to do.

But it wasn't easy to keep her brain from taunting her with a little chant that kept running through it:

One more day.

One more night.

In spite of Emmy's hope for the time she had left with Aiden and Mickey not to pass too quickly, it did.

The morning was busier than usual at the office as she again followed Aiden to take notes. Along with the run-of-the-mill cases of colds and sniffles and flu and other ailments, Aiden examined a man who needed stitches after being bitten by a beaver, another who had to have a bullet removed from his thigh because his hunting rifle had accidentally gone off, and a third whose foot had been caught in a bear trap.

By the afternoon the birth preparation class that Aiden was supposed to teach had turned instead into a bumpy drive to the tiny cabin in the woods, where one of his expectant mothers was in labor.

With Emmy's squeamish assistance as an impromptu breathing coach, Aiden delivered a breach baby that couldn't wait and then turned his SUV into a makeshift ambulance to get mother and child back to Boonesbury to be airlifted to the hospital in Fairbanks.

And then, all too soon, the day was gone and only the evening remained.

Since Mickey was spending the night with Maria, Aiden and Emmy dropped him off there on the way home. Once they had, it was in Emmy's head to tell Aiden she'd rather spend this final evening alone with him. But she was worried that might be too risky after what had happened between them the night before and so she didn't. A nice, safe, homecoming dance was probably a better idea, she told herself, disregarding her other inclinations.

At Aiden's place Emmy went up to the attic room for a quick second bath and to shampoo her hair while Aiden showered and got ready downstairs.

After putting on the wrap dress that was now wrinkle-free, Emmy brushed her hair and left it to fall loose and straight around her shoulders. Because she considered the evening a special occasion, she used a double coat of mascara, slightly more blush than for daytime and a touch darker lipstick.

She'd just finished applying the lipstick when a knock on the attic door startled her.

''Who's there?'' she called.

''Who do you think?'' Aiden said in return, laughter in his tone.

Emmy stepped into her all-purpose black pumps, glanced around to make sure the room was in order and opened the door.

''I didn't know you were picking me up,'' she said as she did, having assumed she would go downstairs when she was ready the way she had every other time since her arrival.

"What kind of a guy would I be if I let my date come to me?" he said as if it were unfathomable. "That'd be as bad as sitting in the car honking for you."

"I see," she said as if he'd just opened her eyes to the custom.

Then she granted herself her first genuine look at him.

He was wearing a suit the way she'd hoped he might, but it so far exceeded her greatest expectations she couldn't help being in awe. This suit had most certainly not come off the rack of the general store, and it was far from baggy or saggy.

It was charcoal gray and fitted him so perfectly it was as if it had been sewn over a mold of his body. And the silver-gray dress shirt and matching tie only accentuated the staggeringly impressive sight he presented.

"Italian?" she asked, after that glimpse of him had nearly made her mouth go dry.

"There's usually a whole table full of casseroles at these things, so odds are there'll be something Italian, yeah," he said, the quirk at the corners of his mouth letting her know he was purposely misunderstanding her question.

"The suit," she amended, anyway. "It looks Italian. And hand tailored." And not what anyone would guess belonged to an Alaskan wilderness doctor.

"I told you my brother Ethan spent a long while

in Europe. Devon and I visited him a couple of times, and when we were in Rome we decided to treat ourselves to suits—for me, a huge splurge. I've never worn this one, but I thought tonight seemed like the time to try it out."

So he had thought of this evening as special, too....

"Well, whatever it cost, it was worth it," Emmy said a bit breathlessly.

Aiden did a slight bow. "Thank you very much."

When he straightened up he studied Emmy from head to toe, smiling his own approval and admiration before he said, "And might I add that you're looking pretty stunning yourself? You're liable to put our homecoming queen to shame."

"Maybe we shouldn't go, then," Emmy joked. Mostly, anyway.

"Not on your life. This is my evening out with you, and I'm not giving it up."

Good answer. It made Emmy smile.

"Maybe I'll just keep this ugly parka on the whole night," she suggested as she reached for her coat.

But as Aiden took the coat from her to help her on with it, he said, "Wouldn't make any difference, you'd still outshine everyone else."

He kept hold of the collar as Emmy slipped into it, leaving his hands there to brush a thumb against her neck.

It was a small thing but it was enough to set off a little tremor inside her, making the previous evening a vivid memory and flooding her with fresh longing.

''The dance it is, then,'' she said in a quieter, sexier voice than she'd expected to hear from herself.

But Aiden still didn't remove his hands immediately. He moved them to her shoulders, squeezing with a firm pressure that reminded her of that first grasp of her breast the night before and only compounded that longing he'd initiated a moment earlier.

Then he let go of her, and Emmy thought it was a good thing she already had on the coat just in case the answering tightening of her nipples gave away just how much of an effect his touch had had on her.

''Shall we do it?'' Aiden asked then.

For a split second Emmy believed he was asking her something else entirely. And she was tempted— so tempted—to say yes, to fling off the coat, take his hand and pull him to the brass bed.

Then what he really meant sank in.

''Sure,'' she agreed, but again her voice was reedy and weak, and she could only hope he didn't notice.

On the way down to Aiden's SUV, Emmy cleared her throat and silently ordered herself to get a grip, using small talk about the dance to help accomplish that as they drove back into town.

When they arrived at the community center, the festivities were already underway. Aiden had been right when he'd assured her that there would be a large turnout of townsfolk.

Emmy just hoped it would help dilute the impact Aiden was having on her tonight.

The buffet dinner kicked off the evening. There

was a long table full of casseroles and salads that everyone helped themselves to.

Dining tables were set up around the perimeter of the room—all of them with seatings for six—so Emmy and Aiden found themselves eating with the minister, the mayor, and their wives.

The homecoming king and queen, and their court, were presented at the end of the meal and then the band began to play and Emmy had to accept the first dance with the mayor.

Her second dance was with the minister, while Aiden winked at her over the minister's wife's shoulder as if to say, Hold on, I'll rescue you as soon as I can....

But for almost the entire evening that was impossible. Emmy would barely begin a dance with Aiden before another of Boonesbury's male citizens would cut in to whisk her away from him.

The worst of these culprits was a high school boy smitten enough with her to cut in a full six times— by Emmy's count.

And even though she told herself it was probably for the best that she was so otherwise occupied, all she could think about was where Aiden was at any given moment and how much she wished it was his arms around her.

It wasn't until late in the evening that Aiden finally took her to dance in a corner, slightly away from the main dance floor, in an attempt to thwart the interruptions.

"I swear if Harvey Lipan comes over here I'm going to flatten him,'' Aiden muttered with a glance at the determined teenager.

''Promise?'' Emmy said, sounding slightly frustrated herself.

''I promise.''

Aiden pulled her close, and if Emmy wasn't mistaken there was something possessive in the way he held her. Something she liked even though she knew she shouldn't. Something she liked a lot.

But she tried not to think about that.

''I was planning to tell you this earlier, but I haven't had the chance,'' she said then. ''I want you to know that I'm recommending Boonesbury for the grant.''

Aiden nodded. ''Does that mean it's in the bag?''

''The decision is still up to the board of trustees, but with my recommendation and Howard in your corner, I'd be surprised if they don't give it to you.''

''Great,'' Aiden said as if it were.

But even so, Emmy had the sense that the grant wasn't the most important thing on his mind at that moment.

Then he said, ''You know what else is great?''

''Hmm?''

''That means the business portion of this is completely over with.''

Emmy laughed lightly. ''I hadn't thought of it that way, but I suppose you're right.''

''And now it's just you and me.''

She hadn't thought of it like that, either. But the idea was so appealing. Especially when it came in a voice that was suddenly more intimate and clearly for her ears alone.

Still, she thought she should try to keep things on the up and up, so rather than commenting on that, she said, "You're a very adept dancer."

Aiden smiled a patient smile, as if he knew exactly what she was doing and was willing to wait for her to get past it.

"The mother in one of the households my brothers and I were raised in was Dunbar's resident dance and yoga instructor. We all learned to do both."

"Dance and do yoga?"

"You should see my cobra."

He said that so lasciviously Emmy couldn't keep from laughing. Or from teasing him.

"Are you sure you don't mean your downward-facing dog?"

Aiden grinned at her. "So you know yoga positions, huh? Well, trust me, my cobra is much more impressive than my downward-facing dog."

She did trust him. For more than his opinion of his yoga technique. And she was already so impressed by him she could hardly stand it. Impressed and as comfortable with him as if they'd known each other for much, much longer.

It was a lethal combination.

But still Emmy tried to fight the attraction and said, "I don't know about your cobra but you dance very well."

"Only when I'm in the corner," he demurred, pulling her even closer so that Emmy had no choice but to rest her cheek to his chest.

Not that she minded. In fact, she was happy to have the chance, and she closed her eyes and just let herself be carried away by the music and the warmth of his big body, the strength of his arms, the scent of his aftershave....

It was heaven, disturbed only once when Harvey Lipan approached them. But Aiden didn't so much as pause to reject the boy's request. He only raised his head from where it rested atop Emmy's and said, "Sorry, Harvey, she's mine for what's left of the night."

It was a comment Emmy thought a lot about as the evening wore on, as the homecoming dance came to a close and Aiden drove them home.

Being his for the night was an idea she couldn't shake.

The business part of this trip was over—that was something else Aiden had said that kept repeating itself in her head—and the remaining time belonged to her. A very short time...

And even though only twenty-four hours had passed since she'd kept Aiden from making love to her, it seemed like an eternity. Long enough for things to have changed.

She was no longer functioning in her capacity as director of the Bernsdorf Foundation. Now she was just Emmy Harris, whose knees were weak from the effects of being with the most attractive, the most charismatic, the most interesting and intelligent, fun and sexy man she'd ever known.

A man she had only this one last night with.

This one last chance with.

And she didn't know if she could let that last chance pass her by....

Emmy was so lost in her own ponderings that she was brought up short when Aiden stopped the SUV in front of the cabin and turned off the engine.

She glanced out the side window as if that wasn't where she'd expected to find herself.

But there they were, home, and she had a decision to make.

Aiden got out and came around to open her door, offering his hand to help her out.

She accepted it just to treat herself to the physical contact and was anything but sorry when he continued to hold her hand as they climbed the steps to the porch.

It had almost become a habit for them to go into Aiden's section of the house. But tonight that wasn't where he led her. Instead, like any good escort, he took her to the stairs that led to the second level, apparently intent on walking her to her door.

"This was nice," Emmy said, wondering if she and Aiden might not be on the same wavelength.

Or if he was just being a gentleman after she had prematurely ended things between them the night before.

"I thought so, too," he agreed as they went up the

second set of steps. "But I'm glad to hear that you enjoyed it."

"I did."

Silence.

This was when they usually discussed what was on the next day's agenda. But Emmy already knew that the next day's agenda was going to take her away from here, and she didn't want to talk about it. Not yet. Not before it was absolutely necessary.

Not before she was sure what she wanted to do tonight...

When they reached the attic door, Aiden stopped and turned to face her, releasing her hand so he could clasp his together at the small of her back and make her his captive.

"So here we are," he said, gazing very intently down into her face.

"Mmm," Emmy responded, trying not to be so aware of every little detail about him. Like the way his arms brushed her sides or the way his hands rode the beginning swell of her rear end. Like how well his aftershave mixed with the pine-scented night air or how extraordinarily handsome he was, bathed in the glow of a full moon.

"Here we are," she echoed, grabbing his tie to hold like a rope and letting the backs of her hands nestle against the solid wall of his chest.

"It's not early," he pointed out as if he were giving her an excuse she could use if she wanted to.

But she didn't use it. She said, "It doesn't seem too late."

Something about that made him smile. "I hope not." He poked his chin in the direction of her door. "We could turn on your space heater and go downstairs for a nightcap," he suggested then, his tone questioning. Testing, maybe.

"We could," Emmy said tentatively.

But she thought about the previous evening and all the other evenings that had come before. She thought about all the evenings that would come after this one when she wouldn't have Aiden there in front of her or the chance she had at that moment. And she thought about the way she felt, the way she felt about this man. She thought about what she really wanted. What her whole being, her whole body, wanted.

And suddenly it wasn't such a difficult decision, after all. In fact, it seemed to be a decision that had made itself.

"Or," she said in a very quiet voice, "we could just stay up here."

Aiden smiled again. A small smile, not an eager one. "Is the timing more right tonight than it was last night?"

"Maybe this sounds strange, but it is. For me, anyway."

His third smile was more open. "Don't expect to hear that it isn't right for me tonight," he warned in a voice that had become sensual and husky.

"I...don't have protection, though," Emmy nearly whispered.

"I can take care of that. Of you," he whispered in return, his breath warm against her ear.

Emmy let go of his tie with only her right hand, reached into her pocket for the key and unlocked the door. She then used her left hand to yank slightly on his tie and bring him inside with her.

But once they were there, with the door firmly closed behind them, Aiden took the lead, removing first her coat and then his suit jacket to drape over the bureau nearby.

Emmy did her part by tugging on his tie until she could pull it free of his collar and toss it on the bureau, too.

"I keep wondering if you were sent to me by heaven or hell," he said with a wicked half smile as he clamped his hands together at the base of her spine again.

"Seems like a little of both," Emmy said.

The room was dark except for the moon's glow, but it was shining directly in through two of the attic's windows, and it was bright enough for her to see him. To see the sharp angles of that face that fed her spirit.

Aiden was studying her, every feature, as if he were trying to commit her to memory.

"You're so beautiful," he said as if he could hardly believe it, making her feel that way. Making her smile a small smile of her own as she gazed up at him.

She looked at his mouth. At his supple lips. Those supple lips she wanted so much to taste, to experience again. She watched them come nearer, nearer, and closed her eyes only when she felt their first sweet pressure against her own.

Slow, slow kisses.

Aiden set the pace. Not a lazy pace. Not a leisurely one. Not as if they had all the time in the world, because they didn't. He kissed her as if he were savoring every press of his lips to hers. Every mingling of his breath with hers.

He unclasped his hands and brought one of them to cup her head, while the other found a place at the side of her waist, and Emmy once again brought her hands to his chest, this time laying her palms there.

She could feel his heart beating almost as fast as hers.

His lips parted and coaxed hers apart, too, to escalate their kisses.

Emmy was only too willing. Too willing for anything, for everything that would bring her into more intimate contact with him.

She kicked off her shoes, keeping her toes curled up, away from the iciness of the planked floor. But the loss of the two-inch heels dropped her lower than Aiden expected and cost her his lips.

"Where'd you go?" he joked.

"Not far," she assured, weaving her fingers together behind his head to pull him back down as she raised up on tiptoe to kiss him this time, to send her tongue to say a scant hello through his parted lips, fluttering against their soft inner edge only to retreat again until his tongue came out to greet hers, to chase hers back into her mouth where he played the game of cat and mouse better than she had.

He managed to dispose of his shoes and socks, too,

as he went on plundering her mouth with his. Then he pulled his shirttails free of his trousers and unfastened the remaining buttons to leave it hanging open down the front.

Emmy seized that opportunity and slid her hands underneath, to his chest again. Only now she got to press her palms to his bare flesh, and the feel of it was so good she just had to have more.

So she followed his rib cage around to his back. She followed the vee of his back as it narrowed to his waist. Then she came around again to his flat belly and completed the circuit up to his broad shoulders and down his biceps, where it took very little to ease his shirt all the way off.

If he looked as great as he felt it would be something to see, and Emmy was itching to have a peek. As wonderful as it was to go on kissing him, she paused to peer at what she'd just learned by touch.

And it was worth it.

The man had an incredible body, and she could have gone on feasting on the sight of him except that he distracted her when he took hold of the end of the tie that kept her dress closed at her left hip and pulled.

That was all that was required to expose her to him—lacy bra, matching thong and thigh-band nylons.

But Emmy suffered only a momentary sense of shyness before Aiden murmured his admiration and dissolved it.

Then he smoothed his hands over her shoulders,

just as she had his, and the dress joined his shirt on the floor.

But the room was cold since neither of them had paused to turn on the space heater, and an involuntary shiver shook Emmy.

In his study of her, Aiden saw that, too, and didn't hesitate to fix it.

He scooped her into his arms and carried her to the brass bed, laying her there and covering her with part of the quilt before he shed those superbly tailored pants and let her see him in all his awesome splendor.

Muscular and toned and perfectly proportioned. He was more than a feast for the eyes, he was a sublime banquet.

And he wanted her. Oh, did he want her! There was no mistaking the long, hard evidence of that.

Then his focus turned to her again, allowing her to continue watching him as he went on to finish the job he'd begun with her dress. He lavished her with the touch of hands that caressed as he divested her of nylons and bra and, lastly, of panties, leaving her as naked as he was.

"*Beautiful* doesn't do enough to describe you," he said, his voice deep with appreciation.

But Emmy was beginning to feel deprived of the feel of him, of his kisses, and she wanted him with her again.

She didn't get what she wanted immediately, though. First Aiden sat on the edge of the bed, giving her only the sight of his imposing back. And when he finally did join her he'd added the only thing they needed between them, fulfilling his promise to keep her safe.

Lying beside her, he recaptured her mouth in hot, sexy kisses now. Kisses Emmy answered with every bit as much enthusiasm, as she let her hands roam again, learning more of the feel, the texture, of every inch of his phenomenal body.

But he only let her have her way for a while before he sluiced both his hands down her arms to her wrists, grasping them to pull them above her head and holding them there as his tongue became more insistent and hers matched his—eager thrust for eager thrust.

He abandoned her mouth to kiss the sensitive undersides of first one arm to her elbow, then the other. Leaving a moist trail to chill-dry and form goose bumps in his wake.

Or maybe it was just being there like that, with him, that gave her goose bumps.

His body skimmed hers as he moved to kiss her, to brush just the tip of his tongue to her shoulders, along her collarbone, to the hollow of her throat. He drew a line with his nose, with his lips, that feathered along her skin, straight down the center of her, then to one breast, nuzzling her there only a moment as yearning grew almost unbearable within her.

Answering that yearning as if he were suffering it himself, he covered her breasts with one strong, powerful hand, returning his mouth to hers and making her back arch off the downy mattress.

He used that arch to slice his other arm behind her, to roll them until she was atop him, lying between his thick thighs, the evidence of his desire a steely shaft just beneath her, nestled against her pelvis.

And yet he was still in command of kisses that grew hungry and urgent and demanding. Of breasts he explored with both hands, kneading and arousing and driving Emmy so wild she could breathe only half breaths.

Then he deserted her breasts, holding her tight against him as they tumbled until he was on top of her, once more kissing her places where his hands had been. To one shoulder and then the other. To one breast and then the other. To her stomach, her navel, her hip bone, all the way down her right leg and all the way up her left, softly—briefly—kissing her where no man had ever kissed her before and then rediscovering her breasts a second time with that wondrous mouth that lingered there now.

Warm, wet, seeking, sucking, flicking his tongue against the taut nipple, tugging at it with gentle teeth.

Emmy lost herself to the sensations coursing through her. Sensations that grew more complex when Aiden's hand began yet another descent, this one to her thigh, to her inner thigh, then up just enough to reach that spot that very nearly put her over the edge when he began to explore the recesses of her.

She couldn't help writhing. She couldn't help moaning. She couldn't help plunging her hands into his hair or raking them down his back.

And then, when she truly didn't think she could wait another moment, Aiden came over her once more, finding the core of her with that thick, rigid part of his own body.

Emmy opened to him, reveling in that moment when he first entered her. When he filled her with that sheathed magnificence. Deeply, deeply within her. So deeply her legs wrapped around his hips almost on their own.

Fully inside her, he brought his thighs up to either side of her hips and used them to support her, to keep himself connected to her, as he raised them both up to sit face-to-face.

His arms came around her, hers went around him, as he started to move, to take her with him on each flex, each pulse of his hips, riding together the tremors that began to erupt, that grew, that swelled, that burgeoned until they became a full quake that shimmered from him into her.

Emmy's head fell backward, and her mouth opened in silent, rapturous agony as her climax held her in its grip, suspending everything for that eternal moment of pure, irrepressible bliss until it was spent, spent in each of them.

Aiden dropped his head to her shoulder, raining hot gusts of heavy air onto her breast, and after a moment Emmy breathed again, too.

And then there was stillness. Satiated stillness.

He eased her to lie back, himself by her side, his big body half covering her as the chill of the air around them cooled the heat they'd generated.

When it had, Aiden retrieved the quilt from where it had fallen to the foot of the bed and pulled it over them, taking Emmy into his arms where she could use his chest as a pillow.

"Are you okay?" he asked her in a voice so raspy she could barely hear it.

"Oh, yeah," she answered, her own voice more a sigh than anything as replete exhaustion overcame her.

He chuckled softly. "Me, too."

Then he rested his cheek on the top of her head, and she felt him relax so entirely she knew he was falling asleep.

Which was exactly what Emmy was succumbing to.

And all without the faintest thought about just how far she was from home.

Chapter Eight

The distant knocking, the faint calling of his name, barely penetrated Aiden's consciousness. After all, he'd had only a few hours sleep. He was warm. He was comfortable. He had Emmy snuggled against his side, her head on his chest, her soft breaths whispers on his naked skin.

But the knocking kept up. From down below at the cabin's front door.

"Aiden? Aiden? It's Maria with Mickey."

Ohhh, damn...

He'd forgotten Maria was bringing Mickey back just before dawn so she and her husband could go fishing for the day.

And here he was, up in the attic room. With Emmy. And without anything to put on except the clothes he'd worn last night.

Great.

A truck horn honked and brought him the rest of the way awake. Maria's husband was probably waiting in the vehicle and getting impatient.

Aiden sighed, slipped out from under Emmy with enough care not to disturb her, and scrambled to pull on his pants, zipping them up as he silently let himself out the attic door.

The temperature couldn't have been more than two degrees above freezing, and the cold chased away any remnants of sleep as he rushed down the stairs to the porch in his bare feet.

"I'm here, Maria," he said in a quiet voice as he rounded the side of the cabin.

He'd only intended to stop her from knocking and calling his name before she woke Emmy, too, but poor Maria hadn't been expecting him from that direction and she jumped.

"I'm sorry," Aiden apologized. "I didn't mean to scare you."

He tossed a wave to his nurse's husband, Ed, where he waited in his truck just as Aiden had figured when he'd heard the honk. Then Aiden took the baby carrier from Maria and opened the front door to let them all into the warmth of the cabin, wondering if he should make some excuse for himself.

But Maria was apparently in too much of a hurry to care because she started talking very fast. "Mickey had a bottle but no baby food for breakfast yet. I changed him, so he's dry, but he's still in his pajamas. And you need to listen to the radio," she said as she deposited the plastic bag of baby gear on the sofa and Aiden set the car seat on the kitchen table.

"The radio?" Aiden repeated.

"I have to go. You know how Ed is about his fishing, and we're already getting a late start. But turn on the radio."

And out Maria went, closing the door behind her.

"Thanks for watching Mickey," Aiden called after her, unsure whether or not she'd even heard him.

Then he focused on Mickey, who was gnawing on a chubby fist. "Morning, big guy."

Mickey gave him a sloppy smile around the fist, almost making it worth it to have had to leave Emmy's bed.

Almost.

"You better give me a grin," Aiden informed the infant in mock warning. "If you only knew what you took me away from upstairs, you'd know you have a lot to make up for."

Mickey answered him with something that sounded like "Goo."

"What do you say we make our Emmy some breakfast and take it up to her? Yeah, some things have changed since yesterday and we can do that now. But first you need out of this snowsuit and I need into a shirt."

Aiden removed the baby's outerwear, replaced him in the car seat, and then took baby and carrier with him to his own bedroom. He set them on the floor and went to the bureau to take socks, sweatpants and a long-sleeved T-shirt from the drawers.

"So what's this stuff about the radio?" he said as he sloughed off his suit pants.

But since Mickey's only response was to gurgle, and that didn't tell him much, Aiden crossed to his nightstand to do as his nurse had instructed and turn on the radio.

The weather report was being read, and as he dressed he listened to it, thinking that maybe they were due for the first snow of the season and that that was what Maria might have thought noteworthy.

But there was nothing in the forecast to warrant interest, and Aiden's mind was beginning to wander back to Emmy as he sat on the bed to pull on his socks.

That was when he heard, "I'm sending out this message every hour on the hour this morning. Hope to catch you one of these times, Aiden."

The disc jockey was talking as if Aiden were in the room with him, and Aiden froze, staring at the radio as the man continued.

"Nora Finley finally heard my pleas and called in to the station. She says the fishing upriver is great and—in case they didn't teach you this in medical school—you have to do more than sleep to make babies, Doc. Mickey may be yours, but not by Nora. She never laid a hand on you."

Whoever was in the booth with the disc jockey laughed in the background.

Then the disc jockey added, "Guess that means we're back to wondering who that little boy belongs to. Anyone with an idea, give us a call, will you?

Doc's probably gonna be needin' somebody to take over pretty quick here.''

Aiden turned off the radio but continued staring at it for a while as what he'd just learned sank in.

Mickey *wasn't* his.

Mickey wasn't his son.

He wasn't a father.

He hadn't slept with Nora Finley and blanked it out.

It seemed as if he should feel relieved. But he didn't. Well, maybe slightly. But more, he felt sad. Mickey wasn't his.

Aiden got up and went to take the baby out of his carrier, bringing Mickey with him to perch on the edge of the bed again. As if the infant needed comforting, Aiden set him on his thigh and held him close, rubbing his tiny back.

''I want you to know that it would have been okay if you *had* been mine,'' he informed the baby, meaning it. ''And there's nothing for you to worry about, you know. I'll make sure this all works out for the best for you.''

In fact, it occurred to him that maybe if no one showed up to claim Mickey, he *would* keep him.

The idea didn't seem like an altogether bad one. In fact, it was pretty appealing. There was nothing that said he couldn't raise Mickey just because they didn't share the same blood. He could adopt him. Maybe that was even what whoever had left Mickey on his doorstep had had in mind.

But *was* that what was best for Mickey? he wondered, as he really thought about it, as he recalled the conversation he'd had with Emmy about this very thing and his telling her Mickey deserved two parents.

He'd do his damnedest to be a good father—that was a given. But would his damnedest be enough?

Maybe not. Not when he thought about nights like the one before last and being called out in the wee hours of the morning. He thought about his having had to wake Emmy to stay with the baby and that if Emmy hadn't been here, he would have had to drag Mickey out of his nice warm crib to take him into the cold. In an emergency situation such as that, Aiden's attention needed to be on his patient, and he would have been forced to neglect Mickey.

That didn't seem like such a good thing for an infant or for a child. As Mickey grew and entered school, rather than attending class after a full eight-hour rest, Mickey could be running on chaotic, disturbed sleep.

No, there were probably other places that would be better for Mickey, he had to admit. And that was what was important—Mickey, and having him in the most ideal surroundings he could be in, with people who could care for him the way he deserved to be cared for.

"Of course, it would be different if I had a wife," he told the baby as if Mickey had been privy to his thoughts.

Yeah, a wife would make a big difference.

A wife like Emmy...

Emmy, who had actually helped him get through this past week.

Emmy, who had been here when he needed to rush out in the middle of the night.

Emmy, who had been ready to fight off a bear for Mickey.

There was no doubt about it, if he and Emmy were to raise Mickey together, it would be a whole different story.

But Emmy was leaving. Today.

And that thought brought on a whole slew of other feelings. Feelings that didn't have anything to do with Mickey.

How was he going to let her go? Aiden suddenly asked himself.

The very idea hit him hard. Harder than finding out Mickey wasn't his. Harder than the thought of giving up the baby.

Maybe he'd been skirting this issue before, but the emotions that were rushing through him were too intense to ignore. And not because of what having her here might facilitate when it came to Mickey. With or without Mickey, Aiden did *not* want Emmy to go.

Even if he ended up having to give Mickey back to parents who eventually showed up again, or to anyone else, he suddenly knew that he would still want to build his life with her. To have other babies with her. To raise those babies with her. He would still want to sleep with Emmy every night, the way he'd slept with her last night. To wake up with Emmy every morning.

"I don't want to lose her, Mickey," he told the baby, the impact of that revelation resounding in his voice.

But no matter what it was that he wanted—and no matter how much he wanted it—he also began to think about some other things.

About Rebecca and how she'd hated Alaska.

About how Emmy had hated it when she'd first arrived.

About how it had nearly killed him when Rebecca had left.

About how just thinking about Emmy leaving now was a knife in his gut and how much worse that would be if it happened after they'd gotten even closer, after they'd built a life, after they'd begun to raise Mickey together, or had kids of their own....

"I don't know if I could take that," he confided, laying his head against the top of the baby's sweet-smelling one.

So what are you going to do? Not even ask? a little voice in the back of his mind demanded of him.

It was a fair question.

Was he not even going to ask Emmy to stay?

It was a possibility.

Because if he never asked, he never had to be disappointed. He never had to be hurt. He never had to hear her say no.

And there was something to be said for all of that. For not putting his heart out there where another woman could trample it.

On the other hand, if he *didn't* put his heart out

where it could conceivably be trampled, he also wouldn't ever have the chance that things between himself and Emmy would work out.

He knew that was what Ethan and Devon would say if they were there, talking this through with him. After all, it had been Ethan who had advised him to let nature take its course with Emmy in the first place.

Still, it wasn't easy to invite the potential for pain.

But then his own thoughts began to echo in his brain.

His heart out there to be trampled on...

The potential for pain...

And he wasn't sure he liked what those thoughts, what that kind of attitude, said about him.

Had Rebecca turned him into someone so gun-shy he wasn't even willing to *ask* Emmy to stay? he had to wonder. Was he so leery that he wasn't even willing to open that door that could lead to what he wanted? To a whole lifetime with Emmy? Maybe with Mickey, too?

That was definitely not the person he wanted to be.

Rebecca might have made him gun-shy, but that didn't mean he had to stay that way. It didn't mean he couldn't move past it so he *could* open that door with Emmy.

So he *could* have a chance with her.

Because otherwise not only was he giving in to something he *didn't* want to be. He was also willingly giving up what he wanted more than anything he'd ever wanted before.

He would be willingly giving up Emmy.

* * *

When the second nip of frigid air bit Emmy's face, she did the same thing she'd done with the first—she burrowed deeper under the covers to escape it, without so much as opening her eyes.

But this time what followed that cold blast wasn't silence that allowed her to fall completely back to sleep.

There was movement.

There was a quiet thunk.

There was a high-pitched sort of half shriek, half giggle.

There was the smell of coffee. Right under her nose, and so near she could feel the steam rising off of it.

She still didn't open her eyes, but she did smile as she remembered her night of lovemaking with Aiden, thinking that now it must be morning and he must be bringing her coffee in bed.

She rolled from her side to her back and finally opened her eyes, surprised to find only the very beginnings of sunrise when she glanced at the window.

"It isn't morning enough for you to be waking me up," she complained.

"I know it," he agreed. "That's why we brought coffee—to make it easier on you."

We?

Emmy looked in the direction opposite Aiden, spotting Mickey in his car seat on the single chair in the corner.

The adorable baby saw her looking at him and repeated the delighted half shriek, half giggle she'd heard before.

"Ah, I see our chaperon has been returned," Emmy said, tamping down a tinge of regret that Mickey's presence meant she couldn't invite Aiden back to bed.

But even the regret was blunted by how cute the tiny boy was as he seemed to flirt with her from a distance, waving his arms and legs at once.

"There's news about him," Aiden said as he poured some coffee from the thermos into a mug.

"What?" Emmy asked, accepting the drink when he held it out to her.

"Mickey isn't mine."

Emmy's curiosity presented itself in raised eyebrows as she sipped her coffee.

"Maria just dropped Mickey off and told me to listen to the radio. Apparently Nora finally called in to the station, and I was right, we didn't do anything that night she spent here. Mickey isn't hers, and if he isn't hers, he isn't mine."

"How do you feel about that?" Emmy asked, having heard a note of something she couldn't quite pinpoint in his tone.

"Mixed, I guess. But it started me to thinking about a lot of things," Aiden said.

He was dressed in a pair of baggy sweatpants and a skin-tight T-shirt that hugged his impressive torso and bulging biceps. The sight made Emmy think too much about having had that torso bare only a short time earlier. About running her hands over every inch of it. Laying her cheek against it. Kissing it…

But she fought the urge to pull the shirt off him so she could do it all again and instead carefully pushed herself to sit up against the brass headboard—making certain to keep the sheets tucked all around her so Mickey, at least, wouldn't know she was as naked as Aiden had left her after they'd made love for the third time during the night.

"What did not being a father start you to thinking?" she asked then.

Aiden sat on the bed beside her, facing her, and took hold of one of her knees from the outside of the quilt, squeezing gently. "It started me to thinking about you."

"Me?"

"I know, seems like kind of a strange progression, doesn't it? But trust me, it wasn't. And what came out of it was me knowing that I don't want to lose you."

Emmy felt another chill, but this one had nothing to do with the attic door opening.

"Am I getting lost?" she asked, forcing a smile this time that she knew couldn't have looked convincing.

"I hope not," Aiden said. "I started to think about you leaving today, about you going back to L.A., about not having you in my life, and I hated that so much I decided I had to come up here and see if we couldn't rectify it."

Emmy set the coffee mug on the nightstand be-

cause she suddenly wasn't too sure she could keep
her hands from shaking.

"Aiden—"

"Just hear me out," he said. "I'm sure what's going through your mind is 'Alaska, he wants me to live
in Alaska of all places.'"

"That's one of the things going through my
mind," Emmy confirmed.

"And I'm not overlooking that you hated it here
when you got here. That, even though you knew you
were going to a rural area, you hadn't expected
Boonesbury to be quite such a backwater and it was
tough to get over just how far from a city you were.
And then there was Mickey left on the doorstep—that
shocked you. And the bear that scared you. After all
that I can't say this was a week to put in the tourist
brochure. But I've watched you, and you've handled
it all. You've adapted when you've needed to. Pitched
in where you could. Maybe even gotten used to some
things—which is more than I can say Rebecca ever
did. So I thought maybe you might consider it."

Emmy's mouth was very dry, and she wondered if
her eyes could possibly be as wide-open as they felt—
deer-caught-in-headlights wide-open. "You thought
maybe I might consider what?" she asked to be perfectly clear.

"I know you need to leave today regardless. That
you have to deliver your report to the foundation.
That you'd have to tie up loose ends and pack, and
do the whole moving thing. But what I'm talking

about is you doing all that and then coming back up here to be with me.''

Before Emmy had had even a moment to digest that, he added, ''You wouldn't have to work, but if you wanted to, I was thinking that there was probably foundation business you could do from up here. I don't suppose you could still be the director—and I know that would be a huge thing to give up after you've worked so hard, for so long, to get the job—but Howard always brings his laptop computer when he comes so he can still keep tabs on foundation business. In fact, a lot of people in Boonesbury work that way. And if you needed to do some traveling to check out areas for grants, there wouldn't be anything to stop you from doing that...''

Aiden was still talking, but Emmy's thoughts were too loud for her to hear him.

He wanted her to move to *Alaska?* To give up the job she'd worked for since she was a teenager. To pack up and live in this wilderness that was so much more isolated, so much farther from civilization than the vineyard her ex-husband had moved her to, that it didn't even seem as if it was on the same planet with civilization. He was talking about her giving up everything. And he seemed to have it all planned. Just like Jon had when he'd come home and announced that he'd bought the vineyard in the first place. All the decisions were made. Aiden was in complete control. And he expected her to just go along...

''No,'' Emmy heard herself say with more force

than she'd intended. Enough force that it scared Mickey and made him cry.

Aiden cut short whatever it was he'd been saying. He squeezed Emmy's knee and stood to go to Mickey.

From Emmy's perch on the bed, she watched Aiden pick up the small baby and hold him gently, patting his back with a hand so big it dwarfed the infant.

In response Mickey curled his little body into Aiden's massive chest, laid his head on Aiden's broad shoulder and nuzzled into his neck.

And as she drank in the sight, something in her whispered, *Aiden, not Jon. This is Aiden...*

But not even that helped. Suddenly Jon and all she'd gone through with him was too vivid. So vivid that it was sending fear and panic all through her to drown out that whisper.

"No," she repeated in a more normal voice once Mickey had quieted. "I went along with someone else making that kind of choice for me once. I left everything I cared about, everything I'd worked for. I was miserable and I ended up hating it. Hating the person who had made those choices. I won't ever do anything like that again."

"I'm not making your choices for you," Aiden pointed out. "I'm asking *you* to make the choice."

"Understand, Aiden, we're two very different people," Emmy said, trying to keep her voice from quavering with tension. "You like rustic living away from everything. But I don't. I only lived fifty miles from the nearest city with Jon—that's nothing compared to this—and I almost went crazy. I felt so totally alone. So cut off from everything. I can't imagine how awful I would feel here.''

''Have you felt awful this last week?''

''No, but there's been a lot going on. And besides, I knew from the start that I'd be leaving. I had a time limit. An out. That wouldn't be the case if I *moved* here. I'd be stuck. Trapped.''

''It isn't as if you'd be in prison, Emmy. Anytime you started going stir-crazy I'd fly you to wherever you wanted to go.''

''That sounds so easy, but we both know it wouldn't be.''

Aiden was rocking Mickey back and forth, still patting his back. But his attention was all on Emmy. ''Does that mean you won't even think about it?''

''Would you? Would you think about leaving your life here, leaving what you want to be doing, what you've worked for, to move to L.A.?''

''Not the same thing.''

''Why? Because you're a man? Because what you do, what you want is more important?'' The way Jon had believed what he wanted and whatever he did was.

''No,'' Aiden answered reasonably. ''Because if I leave, I leave a whole county full of people without medical care—not to mention without the grant money that also wouldn't be awarded to them if they didn't have a doctor.''

''Get another doctor to take your place,'' she challenged.

"There were five years between the one before me and me. And in that time lives were in jeopardy, Emmy, just the way they would be if I left."

His brows furrowed over those deep-set blue eyes of his. Eyes that seemed to see right through her.

"You're putting me in a category with your ex-husband and you're wrong," he said then, guessing correctly what she was thinking. "This isn't me making decisions without you, or taking actions that affect your life without consulting you, or thinking that what you want, what you do, is so much less important. I've thought about this stuff because I'm trying to factor in what you want, what you do. I'm the last person who wants anything less than an equal relationship. I had a one-sided marriage, and it was frustrating and miserable, and it failed. I'm just trying to come up with a solution that will put us together and not rob you of anything."

"In Alaska."

"Yes, in Alaska. Because that's where I have to be."

"And that's also where everything I've done to get where I am goes by the wayside."

"I hope that's not true."

"I couldn't be the director of the foundation here."

Aiden suddenly changed his tack and gave her a one-sided smile that was so charming, so endearing, so sexy, it very nearly did her in. "I was hoping you might be willing to compromise a little if I asked nicely and promised to do everything I could to make it up to you."

Oh, but the man was hard to resist!

And yet Emmy remembered how unhappy she'd been before, with Jon, away from everything. How much she'd come to resent him. How horribly everything had turned out.

And she couldn't surrender.

"No," she repeated yet again.

Aiden closed his eyes and shook his head. "I'm really tired of hearing that." He opened his eyes again and pinned her with them. "So cut it out and instead say you'll at least think about it."

"There's nothing to think about. I let this happen in my life once before and I won't let it happen again."

But there was Aiden, big and handsome and so, so appealing.

And there was Mickey, watching her as if he knew she was about to do something even he couldn't quite believe.

And nothing Emmy had ever done in her life had hurt quite as much.

Yet, despite that, despite the tears that flooded Emmy's eyes, she said, "I just can't."

Aiden looked as if he'd been punched. Hard.

But he only nodded.

And without saying another word, he grabbed Mickey's car seat and carried it and the baby out of the attic room.

Chapter Nine

There were cars as far as Emmy could see in front of her and behind her on the highway. Bumper to bumper. At a standstill.

She glanced at the dashboard clock as she had every few minutes for more than an hour.

It was 7:16 p.m.

She'd left the office at a quarter to six.

Horns blared all around her as tempers flared in the ninety-five-degree heat. Not that it did any good. No one was moving, and there wasn't a single sign to explain why.

Ordinarily Emmy took these things in stride. She'd been in enough L.A. traffic jams to know there wasn't anything else she *could* do. But in the two weeks she'd been back from Alaska she'd been finding it more and more difficult not to join in on the frustrated horn-honking herself.

Of course in the two weeks she'd been back from Alaska she'd had less tolerance for a lot of things. Traffic. Crowds in restaurants, movie theaters and the shopping mall. Lines at the bank and the grocery store. Being put on hold indefinitely on the telephone.

Wait. Hold. Move an inch and stop again. Emmy was sick of it.

The dashboard clock read 7:21.

In L.A., 7:21.

In Alaska, 6:21.

She wondered what Aiden was doing now.

He was probably just getting home.

Was Mickey still with him? Was Aiden talking to the baby the way he did, as if Mickey might answer him? Or were they at the Boonesbury Inn for dinner? Was Mickey being passed around like a football while Aiden shared a booth with friends? Or maybe with Nora Finley, fresh from her fishing trip?

Emmy didn't know why she kept torturing herself with these thoughts. With watching the clock and wondering at all hours what Aiden was doing, who he was with. But she kept repeating the process. Over and over.

And that wasn't the worst of it.

The worst of it were the images her brain flashed at her when she least expected it. Images of Aiden. Images of the way he'd looked just before he'd walked out of the attic room that last morning. Images of him with Mickey in his arms.

It was ironic, really. She'd refused to think about leaving L.A. and moving to Boonesbury to be with Aiden, and yet, since she'd been back in L.A. she hadn't been able to think about anything *but* Aiden and Boonesbury.

Not that she'd thought about going back, because she hadn't.

But she had thought a lot about the peace and quiet of Aiden's rustic cabin. The beauty of the Alaskan landscape. The appeal of the slower pace. The warmth and friendliness of the people. The ease of driving to and from town without another car on the road most of the time...

Emmy hit her horn, futilely adding her complaint to the rest and wondering why things had to be so difficult. Why things couldn't just work out. Why cars couldn't move. Why lines couldn't be short. Why she couldn't stop thinking about Aiden and Mickey and Boonesbury and Alaska...

But for the first time, as she continued sitting in the middle of that logjam, she wondered if—since she couldn't seem to stop thinking about Aiden and Boonesbury—she should give in to it. Give in to thinking about what she'd been trying hard *not* to think about. Give in to thinking about actually going back...

It seemed so radical. So *un*thinkable.

But maybe she needed to take her cue from the course her mind was traveling with a will of its own, anyway. From the fact that now everything in her daily life seemed to be getting on her nerves. The fact that now she couldn't help comparing everything to the way things were in Boonesbury. Comparing and judging Boonesbury superior.

Boonesbury superior to L.A.?

That was more than radical.

But as she sat there, Emmy acknowledged to herself that in some respects it was true that life in Boonesbury was superior to life in L.A. Certainly there wasn't a lot of waiting in the backwater Alaskan town because there just weren't that many people to clog things up. And where there was a wait, it was hardly noticeable because frustration didn't seem to prevail the way it did in Emmy's world. There was more likely to be someone wanting to chat to while away the time.

It was nice.

Although maybe she wouldn't have found it quite as nice had she not been there with Aiden.

That was something she couldn't deny. No matter how hard she tried.

There was just something about the man, something about her feelings for him, that not only wouldn't allow her to stop thinking about him, but that wouldn't allow her to think about him in anything but a positive light. A positive light that shone on everything to do with him. That made even moving to Boonesbury seem less and less like a bad idea.

"So now it's a *good* idea?" she asked herself.

She was on shaky ground and she knew it.

But she went on, anyway.

Was moving to Boonesbury beginning to seem like a good idea?

Maybe.

She certainly hadn't been happy or content in L.A. lately.

In the past two weeks she had hardly been sleeping at all. There hadn't been a single thing she'd found pleasure in. She'd been preoccupied. Her mind had wandered at the most awkward moments—particularly at work. Her job performance was embarrassingly low. And she kept crying unexpectedly—over commercials, over news reports, over the sight of a couple walking down the street holding hands, over a glimpse of a baby in a carrier...

In the past two weeks she'd been more maudlin, more miserable than when her marriage had ended.

And if that was the case, if she was that unhappy being in L.A. without Aiden, was it possible that she could be happy being with him in Alaska?

Oh, yeah, this was definitely shaky ground.

Especially when it meant leaving everything behind as she had when Jon bought the vineyard. When it meant not being director of the foundation. When it meant giving up her whole way of life. Again.

But it also meant Aiden, another part of her pointed out. It meant having a future with him.

And even though that was basically what he'd said that morning in the attic room, now that she'd come to it herself it seemed to carry more weight.

Weight that was beginning to tip the scales in Alaska's favor.

But it was still *Alaska,* the contrary part of her countered.

Alaska...

She'd hated the isolation of the vineyard, and that was nothing compared to the isolation of Boonesbury. She'd felt so alone on the vineyard, away from everyone but Jon. So cut off.

Of course, that might have had something to do with Jon, too, she admitted. Jon who had always been so distant. So inaccessible. So completely involved with himself that he'd barely noticed she was around except for what *he* wanted.

And that certainly wasn't anything like Aiden.

Aiden was warm and open and interested in her, in everything about her.

But she still couldn't get it out of her mind that he hadn't merely asked her to stay with him. That he'd had it all planned out—what she should do to accomplish that, what she should do up there. The same way Jon had.

Well, maybe not the same way Jon had. Jon hadn't had any plans for her except that she should drop everything and go where he wanted to go. After that his only plan for her was to do his bidding. As always.

So she supposed, now that she thought about it, Aiden's suggestions had been just that—suggestions for what she *could* do. And that he'd made them because he *was* thinking about her—the way he'd said.

Which was very different from anything Jon had done.

So Aiden *wasn't* Jon, she thought, just the way she had fleetingly that last morning.

Aiden wasn't Jon in any respect.

And it was true. Now that she really had admitted it, she realized just how true it was.

Aiden wasn't unaware of the needs and wants of other people. He didn't disregard those needs and wants. Aiden had actually been trying to find a way for her to maintain her connection with the foundation if she moved to Alaska, because he'd recognized how important that was to her. That was something Jon would never have done. Something Jon never *had* done.

And also unlike Jon, Aiden was warm and kind and compassionate. He was thoughtful and caring. He had a sense of humor. A sense of fun that Jon had lacked.

In fact, Aiden was more perfect than any man Emmy had ever met.

Except that he lived in *Alaska*.

She kept going back to that. How could she not when it was such a big deal.

Wilderness. Needing to drive a full day or fly in a small plane to get to the nearest city. A general store rather than a well-stocked grocery store and a shopping mall. One restaurant and a take-out pizza place. No movie theater. A library that was in a Laundromat...

And Aiden.

She kept going back to him, too.

In her head at least.

She kept going back to Aiden and the fact that

wilderness and isolation translated into getting to be alone with Aiden. It translated into having fewer distractions from him. It translated into being more focused on each other.

At least that was how it had been while she was there before.

But what about the long term? she asked herself. What about when the bloom was off the rose and they were down to day-to-day living? What about the resentment that had grown toward Jon? Would that same kind of resentment grow toward Aiden eventually?

She weighed that possibility. She tried it on like a new dress.

But in the end she honestly didn't believe she would grow to resent Aiden. Because when she stopped to genuinely analyze her feelings for him, she knew they were just so much stronger, so much more intense, so much deeper, than anything she'd ever felt for Jon.

So how could she come to resent anything in conjunction with Aiden?

And there was one other thing Emmy realized at that moment.

She realized that she wouldn't grow to resent Aiden because *she* was making the choice. Because it was her decision.

So *was* she making the decision to go? To have Aiden?

It seemed as if she was.

And she was making that decision, that choice, for

only one reason—because she wanted him. Because she wanted to be with him. To make a life with him.

So much it actually hurt to think of going on without him.

So much that nothing—nothing—was worth having or doing without him. Not even being director of the Bernsdorf Foundation.

"Alaska…" she said out loud, the full impact of what she was about to do ringing in her voice.

But then she also realized that it wouldn't matter if she had to go to the moon.

To be with Aiden she'd even do that.

The lights were on in the cabin, and Aiden's SUV was parked in front.

"Looks like he's here, so you can just drop me off," Emmy informed the bush pilot who had flown her from Fairbanks to Boonesbury and then driven her to Aiden's place.

The bush pilot was a burly man of extremely few words, and he didn't waste any now. He merely transferred her suitcase from the rear of his truck to the ground, got behind the wheel again and drove off.

Leaving Emmy all by herself.

That was okay, though. She didn't want an audience for what she was about to do.

But she did need to fire up her courage before she did it.

"Maybe I should have called ahead," she muttered, unsure if her desire to surprise Aiden had really been a good one now that she was here.

But she tamped down the dab of doubt she felt, just as she'd tamped down every other doubt that had cropped up over the course of the four days since she'd made up her mind to do this. The doubts only came from jitters, and she was not giving in to them.

The night air was cold and it was beginning to seep through the heavy wool coat Emmy had brought this time. But the chill served as encouragement for her to finally pick up her suitcase and head for the house.

As she did she imagined Aiden opening the door. His eyes growing wide as he realized she was there. Would amazement turn to pleasure then? she wondered, hoping it would, so she could be sure it had been right to come.

But Emmy hadn't taken more than two steps in the direction of the cabin when she saw a silhouette against the curtains that covered the living room window and she stopped to study it.

Was it Aiden who looked as if he'd just stood up, maybe from the couch?

Emmy's pulse picked up speed just at the thought, at the idea that he was so near, that any minute she was going to get to see him again.

But then a second shadow joined the first.

Aiden wasn't alone.

Oh.

In all her fantasies of how this reunion would play out, she'd only envisioned them being by themselves. Well, maybe by themselves with Mickey. Mickey, who she kept hoping would be in their future together. She wasn't thrilled to discover that even though she'd disposed of the bush pilot she was still going to have an audience other than Mickey.

And she was even less thrilled when she saw those two silhouettes come together, back to front, as one wrapped arms around the other...

Emmy's heart nearly stopped.

The shadows were too obscure to let her know with any kind of certainty that one of the people was a woman. But why would Aiden be putting his arms around a man?

Emmy closed her eyes and wondered if she'd just made the most monumental mistake of her life by coming here.

What if she'd tossed everything aside to be with a man who already had another woman? What if her being here just made her the biggest fool in the universe?

Her first inclination was to leave. To get out of there. To run all the way back to L.A., beg Howard to give her back her job and forget she'd ever done anything this stupid.

But there she was, in the middle of Alaska, without transportation or anyone she could call for help even if her cell phone did get a signal.

She was sunk. She was going to have to go up to that house and let Aiden know she was here. And if he was with another woman she would just have to pretend she'd popped in for a visit.

As if anyone would believe that, she thought.

But what else could she do?

Emmy's heart was in her throat, but without any other option, she finally opened her eyes.

The shadows weren't there anymore. There were no signs of anyone through the curtains. But even though she couldn't see anyone, Emmy still knew that they were inside. Aiden and someone else...

With leaden feet she finally forced herself to climb the porch stairs. To go to the front door. To knock...

"Come on in."

That was even worse. The last thing she wanted to do was just open the door herself and go in. Maybe this whole Alaska-laid-back thing wasn't so great after all.

Emmy knocked a second time.

And a second time Aiden's voice called, "Come in."

Emmy debated with herself again, calculating how far it was if she tried to walk into Boonesbury. With a suitcase. In the frigid night air.

And then she opened the cabin door.

Aiden wasn't near the window anymore. And the person he had his arms around was indeed a man. A man whose back Aiden was cracking.

At least he was until he looked up from over the man's shoulder and saw her.

"Emmy..."

"Emmy?" the other man echoed.

"Right on both counts," she joked feebly, feeling so relieved that Aiden wasn't with another woman that she could hardly think straight.

Aiden seemed as shocked as she was relieved, because his arms fell away from his patient and he just stared at her.

It was the other man who came to close the front door Emmy had left open.

Then he stepped around to face her, holding out his hand for her to shake as he said, "Hi. I'm Devon. Aiden's brother."

Aiden's brother...

Emmy took her eyes off Aiden in slow motion, looking at the other man for the first time.

Of course it was Aiden's brother. Emmy had seen him in the wedding video. Although he was even more exceptionally handsome in person. Tall, strapping, gorgeous. Emmy might have had her breath taken away by him except that it was only Aiden who could do that to her.

"Nice to meet you," she said, accepting his hand but unable to keep her gaze from wandering back to Aiden.

Aiden, who looked better to her than he had in all the images of him in her mind these past weeks. Even if he was dressed comfortably in jeans that had a hole in the knee and a plain white T-shirt.

Then, belatedly, he seemed to remember his manners. "Right. This is my brother."

"The wildlife photographer," Emmy supplied for no reason she could understand.

But Devon used it as a segue. "The wildlife photographer who thinks he ought to go into town for a few beers. If he could just get the car keys."

Aiden fished them out of his pocket and tossed them to Devon.

"See you later, guys," he said then, leaving without a goodbye from either Aiden or Emmy, who were still watching each other.

But once Devon was gone, it was Aiden who came out of the trance first.

"You're a long way from home."

Emmy wasn't sure how to answer that, so she didn't. Instead she glanced around the cabin and said, "Where's Mickey?"

"In the bedroom. Sound asleep."

"So he's still here?" Emmy said hopefully.

"For good," Aiden confirmed. "About two days after you left his mother showed up. She's fifteen. Her mom's dead, her dad's an alcoholic, so there's no family support and she's basically on her own. She got tired. Scared. Overloaded. She'd brought Mickey to me when caring for him became too much for her and she'd decided to give him up. The radio announcement got to her, though, and she knew she needed to come forward and formally relinquish him."

"And you still have him?"

"I thought about all the reasons I shouldn't keep him. But in the end…" Aiden shrugged. "I guess we just bonded along the way. He's my son, blood ties or no blood ties. His mother named me guardian and the adoption is in the process. It all worked out."

Just the way he'd felt confident it would.

"Why don't you take your coat off?" Aiden suggested then.

Emmy had forgotten about her coat, but she did take it off.

By the time she had, Aiden was right there to accept it and toss it aside as if to get it out of the way.

He didn't touch her though. He just watched her with those blue eyes. Patiently. Calmly. Then he said, "And why don't you tell me what you're doing up here. Howard already called to officially notify us that we're getting the grant. You can't take it away."

"I didn't come to take away the grant. I came to see you."

"Because you fell in love with me and Boonsebury and you didn't realize it until you were gone," Aiden finished for her as if he'd known it all along.

Emmy smiled up at him. "Pretty much, yes."

"*Pretty* much?"

"I don't know that I'd say 'I fell in love' with Boonesbury. But certainly things about it, on further consideration, did hold some appeal."

Aiden grinned. "So it was just me you fell in love with, huh?"

"Hmm. I don't recall any mention of love," she said to give him a hard time because he was so sure of himself. And of her.

"You gave up everything to come back up here because you just like me a lot?"

"Who said I gave up everything?"

"Didn't you?"

"I could just be visiting."

"You're not," he said confidently.

"But I *could* be."

Aiden raised his arms to rest them on her shoulders. "Okay, you're here to visit. For how long?"

"How long do you want me?"

"Forever."

"Ah," Emmy countered knowingly. "Because *you* fell in love with *me*."

"I did. And I'm not afraid to admit it. Which is what I would have done that last morning if you hadn't barraged me with those *no*s of yours," he said with a devilish smile, as if freely acknowledging that he loved her made him the bigger person.

"Say it, then," she challenged.

"Say what? Emmy, I'm in love with you? I'm glad you're here because I want you to be my wife and spend the rest of your life with me?"

"Yes, say that," she encouraged as if he hadn't.

Aiden played along and repeated it all. Then he added, "Now you say, I love you, too, Aiden, and yes, I'll marry you and stay here with you and we'll have babies of our own—although not too soon—and a whole lifetime together."

Emmy obliged him. Reciting it by rote.

"Now say it for real," he commanded when she was finished.

"I really do love you," she said, saying it as if she meant it. Because she did. With all her heart.

The kidding stopped as Aiden pulled her close, folding his arms around her and holding her tight. "I didn't think this would happen," he confided then.

"Devon has been here consoling me since just after you left, and I think he was beginning to worry that he'd never get to go home."

"I was inconsolable, too. And irate and annoyed over every little thing and... Well, I was just kind of crazy."

"And now you're here."

And now she felt so much better that she knew just how right it was.

"And now I'm here," she said softly.

Aiden sighed, his breath a hot gust in her hair, and for a while they just held each other as if they needed the reassurance of the other's arms around them.

But then something changed, and that reassurance turned into more than reassurance. It turned into something sensual and arousing.

Aiden kissed the top of her head.

Emmy tipped her chin upward so she could peer into his eyes.

Aiden kissed her nose and then her lips.

Emmy's nipples turned into taut points.

Aiden deepened their kisses, mouths opened wide and tongues cavorted. Clothes were shed in a frenzy as mouths clung together. Hands renewed their acquaintance—his with her body, hers with his—exploring and relearning what drove the other wild. Desires were unleashed, erupting and carrying them both away.

Emmy wasn't quite sure how they got there, but suddenly they were on Aiden's couch. Naked and free and uninhibited, coming together in pure, raw passion that first of all rejoined them and then lifted them each to peaks so explosive it was as if their bodies melded and their spirits fused into one to seal their union.

When it was over they lay with arms and legs entwined, spent and glowing.

Aiden laced his fingers through Emmy's and brought her hand to his mouth to kiss her palm before he held it to his rapidly beating heart.

"I love you, Emmy," he said once more in a husky voice.

"I love you, too," Emmy responded.

"Will you really marry me and live in Alaska with me?"

"I'll have to. I handed over the reins as director of the foundation and am now only going to be working on the details of the grants by telecommuting from here. I gave up my apartment. And all my worldly goods will be arriving by truck in three days."

"And here you wanted me thinking you were just visiting. Will you be okay giving it all up?"

"I think I'll be getting a lot more than I've given up."

"Well, you'll be getting a baby, for one thing. Is that okay, too?"

"Better than okay. I was hoping I'd find you both right where I left you. You've made me a happy, happy woman."

"I try to do my best," he said in an innuendo-laden growl. Then he amended his tone to a more genuine one. "Really, I will do anything to make sure you're always happy."

"I know you will."

Aiden squeezed her tight and Emmy molded her naked body to him, laying her head where her hand had been—against his heart.

And as she lay there in exquisite weariness and warmth, Emmy didn't have a single doubt about her decision or the choice she'd made. She loved Aiden, she loved Mickey, too much to have done anything else, and she knew she would never regret trading everything just to be with them.

For all eternity.

Because that was where she belonged—with Mickey, with Aiden, anywhere at all.

*   *   *   *   *

*We hope you'll join us for Devon's story in
June 2003, THE BABY SURPRISE,
the next title in the
BABY TIMES THREE
miniseries, when he finds that fatherhood
could be in his future, too. Along with
love and romance.*

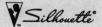

SPECIAL EDITION™

Continues the captivating series
from *USA TODAY* bestselling author

SUSAN MALLERY

These heart-stoppin' hunks are rugged,
ready and able to steal your heart!

Don't miss the next irresistible books in the series...

COMPLETELY SMITTEN
On sale February 2003
(SE #1520)

ONE IN A MILLION
On sale June 2003
(SE #1543)

Available at your favorite retail outlet.

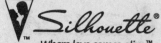

Where love comes alive™

Visit Silhouette at www.eHarlequin.com

SSEHH

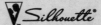

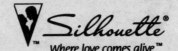

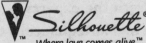